DESPERATION TRAIL

Center Point
Large Print

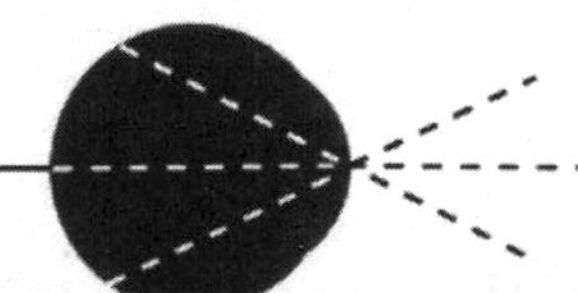

This Large Print Book carries the Seal of Approval of N.A.V.H.

DESPERATION TRAIL

L. L. Foreman

Center Point Large Print
Thorndike, Maine

This Center Point Large Print edition
is published in the year 2017 by arrangement with
Golden West Literary Agency.

First U.S. edition: Doubleday

The text of this Large Print edition is unabridged.
In other aspects, this book may vary
from the original edition.
Printed in the United States of America
on permanent paper.
Set in 16-point Times New Roman type.

ISBN: 978-1-68324-625-1 (hardcover)
ISBN: 978-1-68324-629-9 (paperback)

Library of Congress Cataloging-in-Publication Data

Names: Foreman, L. L. (Leonard London), 1901- author.
Title: Desperation trail / L. L. Foreman.
Description: Center Point large print edition. | Thorndike, Maine :
Center Point Large Print, 2017.
Identifiers: LCCN 2017041670| ISBN 9781683246251
(hardcover : alk. paper) | ISBN 9781683246299 (pbk. : alk. paper)
Subjects: LCSH: Large type books. | GSAFD: Western stories.
Classification: LCC PS3511.O427 D47 2017 | DDC 813/.54—dc23
LC record available at https://lccn.loc.gov/2017041670

ONE

In the breaking pen a pale buckskin horse, long an outlaw and proud as the devil, threw a string of twisting jumps, its back humped up high and its head hung down low and all four feet close together. An audience of ranch hands perched on the top rail to watch. To watch and to pass judgment.

Most of the BJ punchers were Mexicans, hard-bitten vaqueros, brush-busters who didn't mind the wild isolation and crushing heat of the place. Being well below Chisos Basin, the BJ lay only a jump from Mexico. It was easiest by far to run the outfit with a crew of border-bred riders. The brush country of the Big Bend, where the cattle grew up wild as deer and hid in impenetrable catclaw thickets higher than a man on horseback, got on the nerves of Americans and others who were unaccustomed to it. It was apt to give them what Mexicans called the *coraje*: a sullenly murderous turn of mind. Even the border vaqueros themselves occasionally got it.

The rider of the pale buckskin intrigued them. He had intrigued them from the day he showed up and took on to top off a bunch of unbroken jugheads that should have been broken a lot younger. That job done, he set about tackling horses like this brute of a buckskin, animals that had known the saddle but later gone outlaw. Horses could get the *coraje* too.

He was dark, with black hair and high flat cheeks, and spoke Spanish like a Mexican. But his eyes were not Mexican, by color or expression, nor was his manner. Nor his abiding taciturnity, a taciturnity that belonged to a deep quality of reserve and reticence rather than to surly indifference. He spoke only when the occasion called for speech, always quietly, giving never a word more than it warranted. He gave his name as Sam Hatch.

He was tall, but his size had nothing to do with the air of strangeness that hung about him. And it was this strangeness most of all, unseen but keenly sensed, that intrigued the brush vaqueros. The few Americans of the outfit, including the foreman, pegged him as a loner, probably wanted and in all likelihood dangerous if put to pressure. None of them, Americans or Mexicans, approached closer than somewhat carefully civil terms with him.

The only one on the BJ who got anything like close to him was Manuelito, an elderly little Apache who was as sparing of speech as Sam Hatch himself. Manuelito ostensibly did odd chores around the layout for his keep, but soon after the tall man's coming he attached himself to him, shifting his general base of operations from the cookhouse to the corrals. Once or twice the tall man was heard to speak to him in a tongue that was neither Spanish nor English. This gave rise to the conjecture behind his back that Sam Hatch was a half-breed Indian. Sam Hatch was aware of the conjecture.

Each time the pale buckskin hit the ground stiff-legged, the leathers popped, dust spurted like explosions, and Sam Hatch felt the jolt up to his neck. Having tied into a bad one, he would stay with it, but a little of that went a long way. He raked the animal with his spurs to change its style. The horse in its former way of life had known many riders. It had picked up tricks unknown to rough jugheads. It spun a dizzying whirligig. He raked it again, not losing an inch of seat and staying upright in the saddle.

The watching railbirds loosened up to sing out comments, sardonically humorous, intended in their left-handed fashion to express critical appreciation of good bronc riding.

There was one holdout among them, a caustic and distempered American calling himself Colorado Joe. He was a new man, but he had an assertive manner that he made no effort to check, wore his gun at all times, and gave the impression of considering himself several cuts above those around him, Mexicans in particular. For Indians he stated that he had no use whatever. From the first he had watched Sam Hatch narrow-eyed, asking the crew about him.

Sam Hatch knew of it. It always happened wherever he went. Sooner or later some fateful fool always came prodding along. Even this godforsaken end of nowhere . . .

"Call that good ridin'?" Colorado Joe jeered the BJ vaqueros loudly enough for the rider to hear. "You brushy hombres ought to see the real thing. Where I come from we—"

At that moment the buckskin pitched straight ahead, madly bellowing like a steer. It fetched up to the fence and didn't make any move to turn or halt. Colorado Joe piled off the top rail promptly along with the rest, but the crazy animal crashed through the fence and knocked him a dozen yards. Sam Hatch leaped clear of the falling saddle, regretting the ruin of the horse, for he'd had hopes for it. The spilled vaqueros sprang up laughing, but Hatch noticed that Manuelito limped off, as if he had been kicked in the leg.

Colorado Joe didn't laugh over it as did the others. When it came up during the evening meal he glanced at Sam Hatch's black head bent over a plate, and put his words together. "It was kind of an Injun trick," he remarked, and when Sam Hatch didn't take it up he charged challengingly that the tall man had purposely thumbed the buckskin loco into that mix-up because his saddle had got too hot for him.

The talk stilled. Sam Hatch kept his head bent over his plate, as though he hadn't heard the charge. He was indifferent to it, that was all, as long as it didn't dig too deep into the secret thing within him.

Manuelito, though, sitting in the open doorway with his plate, had something to say about it. One word. "Liar!" he grunted, and went on eating.

Colorado Joe shoved back and started around the table for him, drawing his gun and saying. "Here's where I get me an Injun!"

Sam Hatch's rise was swift and without sound. He placed spread fingertips on the table and looked at the would-be Indian-killer, bending slightly forward like a man asking a question, though no words came from him. The occasion did not require any words.

Colorado Joe had been watching him out the corner of his eye on his way around the table. Now he abruptly halted and froze motionless, pinned by the steel-blue stare, shocked by it into forgetting the gun ready in his hand. The silent vaqueros also took in the startling change in the tall, quiet man and sat very still. For this was the very essence of menace.

Yet the change was not actually visible. The lean, dark, flat-cheeked face remained expressionless, the long body not at all tensed, and there were the fingers, the clever fingers, in sight on the table.

The visible change was in Colorado Joe. His face turned sallow and constricted. The cold finger was on him. Presently he walked on heavily past Manuelito and out the door, like a man numbed, the forgotten gun dangling from his hand.

Sam Hatch resumed his seat and finished his meal, still without uttering a word.

The vaqueros later made up a mocking little song about it. The song put Colorado Joe in a poor light, and they sang it whenever he was within hearing.

Before the week ran out, death in a different form reached for Manuelito.

Infection flared in the small gash made above his knee by the kick of the pale buckskin. By the time the old Apache tramp let anybody see it, a sinister streak of red had begun its crawl up his swollen and discolored leg.

The somber Mexican vaqueros spoke hushedly of gangrene, of men they had seen die screaming, and of the will of God. The BJ foreman sent a man riding north to find the nearest doctor, but everyone knew that the red streak would win that race. Manuelito knew it too. Mustering the resources of his racial stoicism, he prepared himself for a damnably unpleasant death.

Sam Hatch, his eyes indrawn and brooding, gazed down at the skinny little figure with its scars of old battles and brawls, for a long time after the others drifted out of the bunkhouse. He knew what he had to do and would do, but he rebelled against it. For here at the BJ layout, at headquarters, riders constantly coming and going and a number of men on hand at all times, it could not be done in secret. Prying eyes and listening ears . . .

Here once again waited the trap, baited with a broken-down old kitchen robber; the trap to lay open the secret thing within him. He could step into it, or he could avoid it simply by turning his back. The decision was already made. He sighed, ending the sigh on a sibilant phrase in the tongue understood by Manuelito.

He carried Manuelito out of the bunkhouse in his arms to the blacksmith shed and spread a wagon sheet for him on the floor. Returning to the bunkhouse, he dragged from beneath his own bunk a canvas sack and lugged it to the blacksmith shed, ignoring the curious stares of those who saw him. He shut and fastened the doors. The shed had no window, and he found a lantern and lighted it. He placed the lantern on the floor, choosing the spot for it with some care.

He unstrapped the canvas sack and emptied it, exposing an Indian satchel of dressed hide, painted—a parfleche, used by the prairie tribes to carry their belongings. Manuelito's monkey eyes flickered at sight of an object so familiar to him.

Sam Hatch saw him raise his head off the floor to study it.

The paint of the parfleche was faded from age, but the designs could still be read. The eagle symbol in green and yellow, emblem of soaring power. The mystic black arrows. The crimson forked lightning. No ordinary parfleche, this one. So proclaimed the signs and symbols.

From the parfleche, Sam Hatch picked out carefully the tools and articles that he needed. Black paint, for the circles. A buzzard's wing feather and a twist of horsehair. The sacred gourd and beads. Four medicine bags. A hollow deer bone and a tube of clay. A quartz crystal. And the indispensable prayer sticks . . .

And a sharp knife. A lancet of finely pointed obsidian. Herbs and roots—he paid particular thought to these, and to the goose quills. Then he stripped to the waist.

Smells mingled thickly in the stifling heat of the closed shed. He squatted beside Manuelito and deftly performed the intricate rites necessary to invoke assistance from the invisible powers. In the yellow light of the grounded lantern his crouched shadow on the wall shaped subtly into that of a sitting wolf, and Manuelito's black gaze shifted to it.

Hatch caught a furtive rustle of movement just outside the shed. Eyes were spying in on him through the cracks between the sun-warped wallboards. The sounds increased. He heard harsh whisperings. He could not stop to do anything about that now, for he was using the obsidian lancet while muttering the *tjahalla* chant, and old Manuelito lay as still as a corpse. Let them stare in goggle-eyed at him in his paint and regalia, damn them, and hear his incantations; it was a rare privilege they had, if they only knew it, of witnessing a medicine man at work.

His enormously strong fingers, still supple despite rough labor with ropes and horses, still clever, manipulated the obsidian lancet firmly yet with infinite delicacy. Then the knife. The cleansing of the wound. Fine powder forcibly blown through the hollow deer bone and clay tube. The precise placing of the goose quills. A loose bandage. Finally, as Manuelito's eyelids fluttered, a last phrase of the low-toned chant:

"*Tsago degi na-le-ya.*"

It was done. Done well. He rose from his heels and straightened up, and the wolf shadow on the wall changed back to that of a man. The whispering outside the shed fell to hissing before fading away. Manuelito moved slightly, breathed a deep sigh, and slept.

He wiped the sweat and painted symbols from his face and torso and removed his trappings. He washed in the water barrel against the anvil. The stale water smelled of iron and sulphur. He repacked the painted parfleche and stowed it into its canvas sack and strapped it up.

Putting on his shirt and hat, he was aware of the silence outside, a complete silence all over the BJ layout, where ordinarily the noises of everyday life only fluctuated between moderate and boisterous, according to the prevailing temperament of the Mexican vaqueros. He threw open the doors of the shed and stepped out into a hushed world of clean air, fresh smells, and blazing sunshine. And staring men.

For a moment the glare blinded him, and he paused, the hot sun striking his cheeks, waiting for his eyes to become adjusted. Then suddenly he got it fully, the feel of standing utterly alone before a pressing wall of antagonism. He thought detachedly of his gun. He was not wearing it. It was hanging over his bunk, and the bunkhouse might as well be a thousand miles off.

From the silent pack of staring men Colorado Joe's voice came at him, weighted with contempt and an acrimonious glee:

"I know you now! I know who you are. You're that Injun witch doctor who tries to pass for a white man. *Shaman Sam!*"

Sam Hatch waited a moment more for sureness of eyesight. All this had happened before, in one shape or other, and by now he knew its force and was not to be swept back by it. The brutal ignorance. The hostile prejudice. Hatred of that which appeared darkly unnatural. The exceptional man, fitting into no common and familiar category, was a monstrosity. Even here, in the wildest depths of the *brasada*, he stood branded as an outcast, dangerous because different from his fellow men.

"White, hell! Black inside as—"

In his precise diction Sam Hatch said quietly across the sunlit patch of yard, "That is enough."

His eyes, that had the hue and glint of newly blued steel, were opaque yet luminous, vitally alive in the dark mask of his face. He was not yet thirty, but most times, and particularly when under pressure as now, he looked as ageless as an Aztec stone image. The Indian look, imposed by long self-control.

And again it was the eyes resting on him that struck Colorado Joe dumb. But this time he had the vaqueros ranged on his side. He had their backing and their moral support. Tough men of the border brush country, none tougher; toward anything smacking of the supernatural they brought the minds of credulous children reared on tales of black magic. The existence of sorcerers went unquestioned. Satan's disciples possessed the evil eye and practiced witchcraft and hexing. Werewolves and *brujos* roamed abroad on certain nights.

Against such imponderable terrors the minds of

the brush country vaqueros knew no protection. They were steeped in superstition down to the deepest abysses of consciousness. San Hatch wondered, not without a certain grim humor, how much of their glowering hostility stemmed from uneasy fear of his presumed powers.

Colorado Joe, with sure knowledge of support, refused to let himself be stared out of courage this time. He shook off the cold finger. “Injun conjure, by God! And him tryin’ to pass himself off for—”

“I said that is enough.”

Sam Hatch paced forward, concentrating his gaze on the man. His step was light, though no lighter than usual. He was able to note the Mexican vaqueros pay special regard to it, as if expecting him to leave the prints of cloven hoofs in the dust. Even his manner of walking took on a sinister quality now in their eyes.

Watching the tall man’s advance, Colorado Joe put his palm on the butt of his holstered gun. He did the act openly, taking his stance. Nobody raised the objection that Sam Hatch was unarmed, though all could see it. This was between man and pariah, not a contest.

Sam Hatch stopped before him. He watched him visibly nerve himself, gather that nerve in a rush, and start his draw.

“You poor damned fool,” he said softly, sparing the words because they seemed needed expending. He whipped a fist to his middle, on the same instant stamping his foot hard down on his instep.

Colorado Joe mouthed a sound between a grunt and a groan, pulling out his gun, mismanaging the draw because thrown far off balance. With smooth precision verging on grace, Sam Hatch chopped the edge of his hand down on Colorado Joe's wrist and the gun spun loose. He caught it, and in unbroken continuation of that sweep he brought the heel of the butt up smack against Colorado Joe's right temple.

He stepped backward several paces, looking over the awestruck vaqueros, who watched Colorado Joe fall senseless. They had never seen the like of that lightning trick before and to them it seemed to have a touch of the supernatural.

Hatch turned and walked away.

The BJ foreman said uncomfortably, and somewhat less than convincingly, "Natchally, I don't put any stock in it, Hatch. Us Americans know better. Evil eye—Damn foolishness. But you see how it is, don't you? *They* believe it. They won't work a lick with you on the place. Where would I pick up another crew this late? Sure hate to lose you—"

Sam Hatch nodded without rancor. He was not tied to his job here and had intended quitting soon. But the foreman, his vague discomfort increasing under the grave gaze, felt impelled to say more.

"Everything bad happened from here on, these Meskins'd lay it to you. That's how they are. You'd have to be all the time on the *cuidado* for a rifle bullet from the brush."

Sam drew his pay. He was readying to pull out when the doctor belatedly arrived. The doctor found nothing much for him to do for Manuelito, who lay behind the cookshack, dead drunk on vanilla extract stolen from the cook. The foreman took the doctor up to the house to have a drink with the owner.

Sam packed and left. He owned a good bay saddle horse and two browns for pack animals. A pretty good outfit for a drifting mustanger and horsebreaker. He did not bid farewell to Manuelito. You did not bid farewell to an Indian, drunk or sober. It offended. As for the ranch hands, none turned out to see him go. He guessed the ranch would settle down to something like normalcy with him gone. It had been up in the air ever since he worked on Manuelito. All work had suspended, and the foreman was frantic.

He rode northward at a slow gait, letting his horses snatch at the sparse bristle grass as they walked. Hurry was not on his mind, nor was the country made for it. The trail through the chaparral, stiflingly airless, trapped heat and held it all day. He had nowhere special to go;

he was becoming soured on this land and its people, and he brooded on the thought that always his lone journeying took him away from somewhere, never toward a known destination. No permanence. But then, he had a task to do, a task that ruled out permanence for him.

He glanced around at the canvas sack containing the painted parfleche, strapped securely to one of the two pack horses. In his keeping, the old parfleche had traveled up and down the border country for six years; and a great deal farther in other hands before his. Determined men, soldiers and federal law officers, had hunted for it when possession of it carried the death penalty. And yet the sight of it quieted his thoughts and restored his solid patience.

The doctor, on his long return trip home, caught up with him on the edge of Dagger Flats, where thousands of tall yuccas, not yet flowering, stood like lances protruding straight up from bunches of sharp green sabers. He reined down the lathered team of his dusty buckboard, driving alongside Sam Hatch and offering a greeting. His name was Dwyer, and he was originally from somewhere East, and why his card had got shuffled down to this deck-bottom country was anybody's guess. The guess was drink.

"I welcome an excuse for a run down this way," he confided presently. "This part of the country is so weirdly wild, makes me feel Marfa's halfway civilized by comparison. Makes me halfway content with that miserable town for a while. Only for a while. The people down this way are wild too. Wild-crazy, like their cattle and horses. I use the term 'people' loosely. They're savages. Are you an Indian?" he asked, and at the tall man's curt headshake he commented, "You don't have the eyes. Still, they called you Shaman Sam on the BJ. A shaman's a witch doctor, right?"

"Ask the wild-crazy ones."

Dwyer ducked his head humorously, as from a blow. "Gr-rr! It's only my professional interest. What I'm leading up to say is, you did a neat job on the old Indian's leg. Never knew of goose quills being used for surgical drainage before. Must remember that. You obviously understand the main principles of treating infected wounds. Why, then, all the hocus-pocus they told me about? God, to hear those Mexican wild men talk—"

Sam offered him no reply. He considered pushing on ahead. The pertinacious doctor had a fast team, however, while the pack horses were slow, steady animals.

Holding his team in, Dwyer observed musingly, "A white witch doctor, in this enlightened year! Devil worship. Black magic. Incantations and sorcery. Well! I can understand our Mexican bushmen friends taking in such mumbo-jumbo, yes, and it scaring 'em bug-eyed. What gets me is finding an intelligent man who actually practices it. It's fantastic. Tell me, Shaman Sam—"

"My name is Hatch," Sam interrupted in a flat tone that brought the doctor's head sharply around. "I'll trouble you to call me that. Better still, drive on."

"My apologies, *Mr.* Hatch," said the doctor, dryly polite. He let his team out and bowled on out of sight.

But when Sam Hatch pulled into Palma Canyon that evening, there was Dwyer camped for the night at the spring, and the next water no nearer than Forty-Mile Post. He must have made an early halt, for his cookfire was not new and evidently he'd had time for some healthy whacks at an uncorked stone jug.

He hailed Sam Hatch expansively, jovial on the jug, imitating a cowman's greeting. "Hahdy, pahdnah! Light an' share chuck."

Sam unloaded and watered his horses, staked them out on a scatter of grain, and joined the doctor at his fire. Dwyer waved him to the jug.

"Try that on your flue. Guarantee it's more potent than witches' brew stewed in a cauldron under the blue moon. Which reminds me. Something I'd like to know. Professional interest, purely. What else did you use on that Indian's leg besides the knife and magic? In the way of medication, I mean."

Sam lifted the jug and drank from its mouth. The whisky was still warm from the day. Going down, it bit hot. "Rhatany root, burdock, dogwood bark. Other herbs I know only by Indian names. Dried and powdered."

"Goddam effective," Dwyer commented. He thought for a while. "Botany is the basis of all the medicine I know of. But they say you put him to sleep while you operated. Made him dead, is what they maintain, then brought him back to life. Don't tell me you know what chloroform is."

"No. Yellow wolfsbane, hyssop—and something more. *You* call it incantation."

Dwyer raised his eyebrows. "A kind of mesmerism, is that it? Monotonous repetition, helping along the action of a sleep-inducing drug. The patient is made to believe he feels no pain. You don't mind telling me your secrets?"

Sam Hatch smiled faintly, setting the jug down. "Any medicine man worth the name knows those things."

Dwyer sat down by the fire, within easy reach of the jug. He nodded sagely. "They're not exactly secrets, no. Herbal remedies—well—" He drew the jug to him and lifted it. "They're as old as man, I guess. And your mesmerizing technique is nothing new. Still, you have to learn those things. I'm not belittling, y'understand."

He drank deeply and put the jug back. "You *are* a shaman?"

". . . I was," Sam said slowly, sparely. He could not unlock his tongue to talk of himself, and he moved around the fire and sank onto his heels.

And then the hideous loneliness enveloped him. As so many times before, it descended upon him with no warning whatever, and he stared impassively into the fire, waging his inner battle. To the doctor's attempts to reopen the discussion he made no response, and shortly Dwyer set about the meal.

After they ate he began to relax. The night was pitch black, stars were white beacons, the fire a kindly hearth to the spirit. A faint breeze sprang up to wipe out the wood smoke and cool the air. He found that he was amused, not irritated, by Dwyer's renewed attempts to draw him into conversation. For once he didn't mind the company of a talkative man, partly because the doctor talked knowledgeably of places and matters afar from the border country.

Doctor Dwyer had an egg-shaped face, exaggerated by a bald head and pointed beard. His features were crowded into the lower part, leaving a great deal of pale and empty expanse above. The effect was top-heavy and gnomish, and as he continued drinking from the jug his eyelids drooped and he developed a Chinese cast of countenance.

"I venture the opinion, Mr. Hatch, that your,

er, medical training was unconventional, to say the least." The drinking was making his speech formal and uncertainly elaborate.

On rare impulse Sam let down his reticence. "I was taught by a great medicine man, perhaps the greatest," he replied deliberately. His tone softened. "He was a Sioux of the Oglala."

"A Sioux! Way down here? Long way from home, wasn't he?"

"Yes, a long way. His name—" Sam hesitated, mentally shook his head to a tiny warning voice, and gave it. "His name was Tasunke-Wankantuya. The whites called him Tall Horse. He was my father—"

Dwyer's heavy eyelids opened wide. "Tall Horse!" he snapped, and then checked it with a quick cough and changed it to, "But if you're not Indian—"

"My foster father," Sam corrected.

"H'm." Dwyer was not nearly as drunk as he had been a moment ago. "You must have quite a story to tell."

Sam nodded. "If you'd care to hear it." He found it easier to talk now. "I don't know all the story. I was only seven when my father—he was a cattleman—decided on a change of location. There had been a long drought where we were, along Devils River. We were moving north. I remember talk of leasing Indian range and a place called, I think, Desperation. That's where we were headed for. It sounded exciting to me, a kid, with that name."

"Never heard of it," Dwyer murmured.

"Wherever it is," Sam said quietly, "we never got there. A band of Indians jumped our camp one night. We were camped on a creek, a long way up north. Or it seemed a long way we'd gone, to me. My father had said that day that we weren't far from our destination, only three or four days more. He was killed, I think, before he could reach a gun. My mother and my sister fell at the first shots—"

"Didn't your crew put up a fight?"

"They weren't there. There was just us. My father had sent his foreman ahead with the herd and outfit early in the spring to establish the new ranch. There was some business to wind up before we could follow, in a wagon."

"You *think* the foreman was killed?"

"That's a part of the story that's missing. I don't know. I got hit in the head, and they left me for dead. Some other Indians picked me up later, wandering. I wasn't right in the head, and you know how Indians are about people they think are crazy. I don't know how often I was traded from band to band and different tribes during long treks, before Tall Horse bought me."

He spoke of it in matter-of-fact tones, as another man would reminisce of a normal boyhood, causing the doctor to gaze at him incredulously.

“What Indians were they that jumped your camp?”

“I don’t know. A gang of Tonk tramps, most likely. They wore white men’s castoffs. It was about twenty years ago, in the northern part of Texas somewhere.”

“That’s not much to go on,” the doctor commented. “Those gangs of Indian renegades and mixbloods have been chased out of Texas since then.”

Sam nodded patiently against his pinching thumb and forefinger. “Most of them ran for the border. What’s left of them can still be found in the brakes and thickets. It’s for that reason I’ve been scouring the border country these past years, living in their hideout camps wherever I could find them, keeping my ears open. Trying to find someone who remembers that night.”

Now that he studied him, Dwyer perceived the scars of past violence on the dark, lean face and wondered how many murderous fights this quiet-voiced man had survived in those outlaw hangouts. He asked, “Pick up anything?”

“Nothing but a reputation. Among the border bloods I’m a white Indian. Among white men I’m Shaman Sam, regarded as a half-breed. I found nothing that I looked for. Not a whisper.”

The doctor considered. “I should think,” he began, “the name of Hatch—”

“My Sioux name is Hache-Hi,” Sam said.

"I changed it to Hatch. Tall Horse"—his tone altered as before—"gave me that name when he took me as his son."

"Tall Horse, the old recalcitrant," Dwyer muttered. "The Sioux chief who refused to come in at the surrender. The old devil who skipped clear down to Mexico with a diehard band of warriors and defied the army to catch him." He met Sam's sharp upraise of face and stare squarely and let his eyelids droop again. "I was a contract surgeon with the army at the time," he explained.

"There were few warriors with us on that long trek," Sam said harshly. "Few men. Women, yes. And children. We were not a fighting band. We were fugitives. Tall Horse was a great medicine man, respected. His prestige was high in all Indian councils. But he was never a warrior chief."

Dwyer blinked. "The army can go wrong, God knows," he admitted. "The word was that they were hostiles, a tough bunch hand-picked by Tall Horse, warrior chief who hoped someday to rise again. It wasn't doubted. Goddam, they *had* to be tough to slip through all the traps the army laid for 'em! We knew Tall Horse had his son along. I never heard it questioned that his son was Indian. Did he have another?"

"Tall Horse had no children of his own. He looked on me as his son. He was my father and my teacher. As long as he lived I was Indian. But after he died—"

"I see." Dwyer nodded slowly. He reached absently to the jug and let his hand fall. He looked across the fire at the man sitting so still and seemingly in such complete control of himself.

"Give up your search, man," he advised. His eyes were all at once surprisingly gentle. "Head north. You're a white man. *Be* a white man. Oklahoma would do. I could be persuaded to go with you, Hatch. That"—his eyes shifted to the stone jug—"may be my salvation, too. A change of country— How about it?"

"It has been on my mind to go north," Sam said. He stared into the fire and sighed faintly. "But first I have things to do across the border. It was the wish of Tall Horse that I father children. So he bought me a wife. We have a little daughter. I haven't seen them these six years."

Dwyer flattened out a hand, palm down. "Forget 'em. An Indian marriage doesn't count for much with a white man."

"It counts with me."

Shaking his head impatiently, Dwyer stated, "You've got to throw all that behind you! Let's go north to Oklahoma. And when we get there, don't you ever let out a word to anybody of what you've told me. I mean about you and Tall Horse!"

Sam raised his gaze from the fire. "If I threw the woman and child behind me," he said with utter reasonableness, "it would do me bad, inside." He searched for further words to make his meaning clearer and found an analogy. "It would be like using my medicine for a bad purpose. My medicine would turn against me."

"My God—nature's nobleman!" Dwyer muttered, and now he had to swallow a hasty drink. Setting the jug back, he exploded, "Your medicine! Goddam it, be sensible! Herbs are just herbs. The rest of what you call your medicine—what is it? Flummery! Paint and feathers and fixing yourself so your shadow looks like a wolf! Oh, they told me about that too."

Unperturbed, Sam said, "The wolf is my symbol. Manuelito recognized it. Without it, and the other things I did, he would never have believed he was cured. He would have died."

"That's possible," Dwyer granted, shrugging. "The human mind is damned queer. My point is, *you* know it's all fake."

"Not all." Sam's eyes were unreadable.

The doctor shifted uneasily, hunching his narrow shoulders. Sam upset him. He could not reconcile this reserved and solitary man with what he thought of as gaudy charlatanism.

For Sam, on his part, it was impossible to put into words the things that he knew and had seen and felt. The secret language of symbols. The understanding, learned in flashes during periodic retreats into solitude and long fasts. The quiet splendor of the inner life and its mysteries and creative freedom, of which the techniques and practices of shamanism formed but a small patch of outer manifestation.

Under the guidance of Tall Horse, mystic and healer, the meaning of the web of life—soil and minerals, water, forests, animals, and mankind—had been made known to him. Man simply was a partner in the living world, collaborating with it, respecting it and himself, sensitive always to unseen forces, tranquilly accepting any hardship imposed upon him by *Wakan Olowan*.

His conscious mind Sam could control as well as Tall Horse could teach him. He had never learned to discipline his heart.

Shaking off his exasperation, Dwyer said banteringly, "That old devil of a Tall Horse worked a spell on you, boy. How long has he been dead?"

"Six years."

"Ah. Six years. And that was when you started out on the long prowl, looking for the Tonks who massacred your folks. To kill 'em off, one by one, eh?"

"To question them," Sam corrected. "To force them to tell me what I want to know." He paused a moment, and went on. "After I was hit, there on that creek, I came to for a few seconds. Our wagon was fired, burning at one end. My father was carrying considerable money, in gold. In the wagon. I heard a man cursing the Tonks for firing the wagon too soon. *He cursed them in English!*"

Dwyer's top-heavy countenance went slack with horrified repulsion. "Goddam!" he grunted deeply. "A white man! They were led by a white man then!"

Sam rose and went to spreading down his bedroll. "Yes," he murmured. "A white man, one who somehow knew of the gold in the wagon. *He* is the one I want. He may be dead by now. I hope not. I want the pleasure of killing him, if I can ever learn who he is, if I could learn his name . . ."

The doctor, just before dropping off to sleep in his own bedroll several drinks later, remembered that Sam Hatch had not told him his own real name, the one he was born with. It was wise of Hatch, the doctor reflected, to keep it unspoken. A man couldn't be too careful, tracking an unknown enemy. Tomorrow he would ask him . . .

But when he woke up late next morning Sam Hatch was gone.

TWO

The odor met him on the soft night breeze from the south while he was threading his way through remembered low hills that were studded with rock and malpais and overgrown with pear cactus. The moon was nearly full, so radiantly bright that he could see by its light that the narrow trail underfoot had not been in use recently, which surprised him. Recollection insisted that the permanent camp of the Sioux exiles lay not too far ahead. This was a regular trail straggling out from it and should have shown the signs of comings and goings.

He would not have approached the camp by night, except for a heavy rain that afternoon, the little band of Sioux in their exile being as distrustful as thieves in hiding and the women as prompt to shoot as the men. The women, far outnumbering the men of the band, had perforce become, in a sense, warriors, defenders of the hidden camp. The afternoon downpour, forcing Sam to take such shelter as he could find, had allowed his horses a rest. They were still fresh enough at sundown, so he had obeyed the bidding of a restless mood and pushed on.

The lack of travel sign along the trail bothered him. It could mean that the Sioux had abandoned the old site for some reason. Somebody may have had a dream of strong warning. Perhaps signs and portents had visited them, making a move imperative. Or, more concretely, a visit by Mexican soldiers, although in his time here Sam had never known soldiers to patrol this rough and lonely stretch of country close under the border. Nothing existed here worth official notice, which was why Tall Horse had chosen it as the place where he would guard and nurture his remnant of Sioux independence.

At first the odor came faint, a mere rumor of a smell that strengthened as he rode on into the low breeze. Its intrusion brought to him an awakening sense of the familiar and what he first took to be a nudge of foreboding. The horses upped heads, snorting softly. Their eyes shone in the moonlight. The smell was evil.

Somewhere along his advance the familiarity of it came rushing upon him like a mysterious shadow emerging from an almost forgotten nightmare of childhood, and next it silently exploded a picture before his eyes, a ghastly remembrance of many dead.

They had been, he thought, Arapahoes. He seemed to recall lodges of buffalo hide painted with much artistry, and intricately bead-worked dresses. And talk of the sun dance. Yes, Arapahoes, of course. It was difficult to remember everything right off. He had lived as a semi-captive boy with so many of the tribes—palmed off from one to another—and trekked so far with some of them, before Tall Horse bought him and cleared the fog from his head.

It had been far north, long ago, at a place where columns of white-topped wagons swayed past to vanish slowly westward over an endless plain. A dread sickness had struck the people of the painted lodges, and the dead and dying lay everywhere, untended. The survivors, living skeletons, crawled about aimlessly, dazed and without hope. And over all hung the smell, that pervading smell.

A white man from a passing wagon train, implored upon for help, came and spoke fearfully of something he called cholera, the Asiatic cholera, one of the curses brought by white men to the plains. The man had hurried away, handkerchief to mouth and nostrils, and the sickness ravaged on unchecked until at last *Wakan-Tanka* took pity and sent a thunderstorm and deluge that drove it off. . . .

The bay saddle horse balked, snorting more loudly. It communicated its apprehension to the two stolid brown pack horses and they hung back, tucking in tails and rolling eyes in fear. Sam jerked at the lead ropes. Subdued but nervously high-stepping, the animals clomped onward against the thickening stench.

On the overlooking bluff he drew in, staring

downward, chilled to the heart. This had been his home. In this lonesome place he had counted as a member of the little band that chose bitter flight to poverty rather than suffer the indignities and beggarly handouts of a Government reservation.

A group of them huddled in the open *hocoka*, center of camp, where they must have gathered to offer a forlorn last medicine song before death overtook them. Others lay about the camp where they had fallen or crawled.

The flaps of the high-peaked pole lodges hung open to the moonlit night. No glow of banked fires showed within. The low breeze from the south captured no wisp of smoke. Among the littered settlings of bones and clothes-shreds slunk snarling gray shapes.

Sam descended the steep path slanting down the face of the bluff, heeling the reluctant bay mercilessly. He let go of the two pack horses and drew his six gun and fired twice into the air. The two shots rattled enormous reverberations from the bluff, instantly scattering the gray coyote pack. A cloud of ravens rose screaming from a gaunt stand of leafless cottonwoods, followed silently and ponderously by hundreds of buzzards. A weak, keening cry cut thinly through the raven fury.

As he crossed the stream below the bluff, he noted its fullness and the muddy quality of its water. New rain. The downpour of this afternoon, then, which had delayed him, had also swept through here. This was a land of long droughts broken by sudden deluges of brief duration. The rains ran off the concrete-hard earth, gushing down flooded arroyos into the wasted nowhere, but some seeped in to bring fresh life to the soil. The stand of dying cottonwoods would revive and leaf out to discourage the carrion birds. Buzzards preferred to do their roosting in dead trees.

He passed through the soundless camp, walking the bay from side to side, vainly seeking some movement of human life. The bay shied from a withered crone seated against a tree stump, still clutching a bundle. The bundle had been a child. The crone was dead.

In the bright moonlight the ravens returned, quarreling hoarse-voiced for positions as they clustered. The buzzards, effortless flyers on high in the sun, ungainly on earth, half-blind in moonlight, glided back and awkwardly fluttered and flapped to roost. The coyotes yapped and howled sullenly, prowling the outskirts.

The people would never revive as would the cottonwoods. They were all dead.

He halted south of the camp, the windward side, and he dismounted and stood by the trembling bay horse. He bowed his head.

His Indian wife, Nabilase, and his half-Indian

child, Naka—which of those among the coyote-torn shapes were they?

Dead. His grief, honesty forced him to confess to himself, was less than shattering. Six years had passed since he saw them. It had been Tall Horse who dictated the choice of Nabilase and correctly purchased assent from her father, an Arapaho, a man of temper who had joined the fugitives with what remained of his family.

Sam had taken Nabilase willingly enough. He was young and virile, and she was ripe. The child was born the first year, a girl, a disappointment to Tall Horse, as he made plain. Too many females in the camp as it was.

Now he was released. Imbued at the time with the Indian point of view toward females, he had spent only a guardedly aloof affection on little Naka. He had trouble now in recalling the looks of them both, mother and child. For Tall Horse he retained sharp memory. Tall old man, lean essence of dignity. Black eyes, forceful yet tolerant. The proud stare that surfaced over the remote gaze of a mystic.

He was free. Free to trek north and find another country and be a white man among whites. No knifing conscience. He stared down at the ground, forgetting the guilt of self-interest in the thought, then raised his eyes to the moon, pale wife of the sun.

The moon sank westward, obediently following

her spouse. Long shadows of misty blue-gray spread from the bases of the tall conical lodges. The coyotes crept back. Sam quivered. He fired his gun, driving them off. The ravens and buzzards soared a brief, grudging flight. Through the harsh cawing he heard once more the weak, keening cry. Not an animal cry, or at least not the cry of any animal he knew. Human then, perhaps. He left the bay horse with reins grounded and went searching on foot.

He discovered them atop the talus rock and rubble that past ages of rains had washed loose and heaped up at the foot of the bluff: two cadaverous females in rags, crouching, arms entwined pitifully about each other, under a filthy blanket.

One was a child in size. She kept her head pressed hidden against the other one, like a terrified kitten tucking itself under its mother. The woman mouthed a sound up at Sam. He could not tell whether it was a moan of thankfulness or a threatening growl. Her hair hung over her eyes, and her face, what he could see of it, had shrunken beyond the ability to express anything like a human emotion. The shivering child barely breathed against her.

In an effort to pacify them he said, indicating himself by tapping a finger to his chest, "Hache-Hi—"

In that thin, keening wail that he had heard before, the woman echoed, "Hache-Hi!" and rocked her body to and fro on the ground. Then, suppressing that grotesque display of emotion, she mumbled, "Wicapi—"

He could not recall her. There had been a younger sister of Nabilase named Wicapi, a dreamy little creature whom nobody ever noticed much, but no woman of that name. He guessed that the poor half-crazed creature was trying to tell him of his family, because next she whispered, "Naka—"

"Nabilase?" he asked her.

But she fell into a stupor, peering blindly up at him through her strings of hair, mouth agape. Her eyes disturbed him. And he sensed something else about her, an anomalous something the nature of which eluded him. That she knew him, or recognized his name, her eyes left no doubt. The mute stare, fixed on his face, contained unutterable relief.

"*Imaku wapi lo . . .*" He bent and gently touched her and the child. "I help you."

They were pathetically thin, so light that he was easily able to carry them both in his arms down the talus slope and through the dead camp to the waiting bay horse. He then climbed the path up the bluff and brought down the two pack horses. He unloaded the animals and made camp. He unpacked the old painted parfleche and, without feathers and paint or chanting, set about doctoring and nursing the two females. He built a fire, cooked a broth from jerked beef to which he added a few selected herbs and roots for stimulant, and spent over an hour patiently spooning it little by little into their mouths.

The woman's teeth were small and even, white. Young teeth. That, he supposed, was what had bid for his attention when her mouth had fallen agape. Her body, though terribly wasted, was a young body. He heated water from the stream in an iron cookpot from the camp and washed her and the child, bundling them then immediately in his own blankets.

Their clothes he burned in the fire. Tomorrow he would ransack the lodges for others and wash them thoroughly. And some blankets and other articles. He sat guard over them sleeping cuddled together under his blankets. His eyes, playing over their relaxed faces, grew brooding. The two already looked more human. The child, he judged, was about seven years old. The woman that he had taken to be an old hag, he knew now, could be no more than eighteen. He thought of the two names that she had spoken, and he studied the two sleeping faces more closely.

He knew now with some certainty who they were. The child was Naka, his daughter. The woman was Wicapi, young sister of his Arapaho wife, Nabilase.

Again an unbidden thought, cast in guilty self-interest, intruded itself.

He was *not* free. . . .

Manuelito rode down the bluff four days later on a red roan gelding, packing a Winchester repeating rifle. About him still clung a faint effluvium of vanilla extract. Sam recognized the horse and saddle as having belonged to Colorado Joe last time he saw them. Also the Winchester.

"Brother," grunted Manuelito, pulling up at camp.

No earthly use to argue with an Apache of the old blood when he claimed you as a brother. And just as useless to ask him how he found his way here. He'd answer that he followed his spirit or his nose or something of the kind. And he'd believe it himself, because trailing came so naturally to him that he did it with no conscious thought. As for the stolen horse and rifle, that was strictly his own affair.

Sam, hollow-eyed from lack of sleep, merely said to him, "Keep the fire up. Give these two drink from the small pot whenever they ask for it."

Manuelito cast a cold eye down at the females. "Why?"

A reasonable question. "Because," Sam told him, flopping down to sleep on the bare ground, "they are my family. Therefore," he added as a clinching afterthought, "they are also your family."

He had learned by then, from Wicapi, the story of the disaster. It had started with the arrival of a sick white man, a prospector, who wandered into the camp of the exiles. The weather was unbearably hot. For a very long time no rain had fallen. Even the air smelled of scorch, and the stream had dropped to a trickle.

Those who touched the sick desert rat were the first to be stricken, soon clasping their stomachs, collapsing, dying. Within a day and a night the evil scourge was raging through the camp, and the people were in panic.

"We no longer had Tall Horse to drive it out," said Wicapi. "Nor you, Hache-Hi—"

The white man appeared to be recovering amid it all. So they cut off his head. It didn't help. The people possessed no shield against this dreadful thing, no immunity whatever. When it struck it killed, sometimes in the same hour.

All work and activity ceased. The life of the camp came to a standstill. The few still living dragged themselves to the *hocoka*, there sang medicine songs to the end. Then came ravens and buzzards, more and more of them, blackening the trees and the earth. Then the coyotes, a horde of them, big gaunt beasts with slanted eyes flaming yellow fire.

Soon after the beginning Nabilase died, and

Wicapi had taken Naka, child of Hache-Hi, up the talus slope away from the camp. Wicapi could not say why she did that. Something had told her to do it. A dream, perhaps, since forgotten. Wicapi had always been a dreaming kind of girl. Or sheer instinct. Or a dim memory of advice spoken by Tall Horse, who had known a thing or two about the white men's plagues.

She carried up a store of food, and for a while she and Naka subsisted fairly well, nobody bothering them while the dying went on. Water she drew from the stream below, obtaining it at the nearest spot which was above the stricken camp.

She—not much more than a child herself—mothered Naka, crooned made-up songs to her, held her tight through the ghastly nights. She comforted her with fanciful tales of her father, Hache-Hi, whom the little girl did not remember, and described how he would return to save them.

She did not despair, Wicapi insisted earnestly to Sam, until the food ran out, and she crept down to the camp to forage for more while Naka slept.

The coyotes . . . they held the dead camp. They were drunk on feasting. Drunk on ptomaines. Their fierce rapacity knew no bounds. They glared boldly at her in the darkness, refusing to give way. They knew she was only a female and alone and unarmed. She was as vulnerable to their bared fangs as any young doe that they had ever harried and pulled down.

She retreated back up the talus slope. Many times more she tried with desperate resolve in the days and nights following, always with the same result. Naka cried with hunger. Wicapi made one last try, failed, and after a while Naka cried no longer, held in Wicapi's arms. Came the day when Wicapi found she was too weak to go down to the stream for water.

"I truly tried, Hache-Hi! See my hands. See my knees." She was painfully anxious that he should believe she had done her best and forgive her for not doing better for his child.

"I see, little sister."

"Hache-Hi, you sent the rain too late." She was sure it was he who, coming home, had sent the rain on ahead to bathe the barren hills, sluice the arroyos, and scour the camp clean. She *knew.* "Too late to save the others." Her rebuke, if it was a rebuke, was timid.

The rest were dead and nothing remained to hold him to the border country. From the devastated camp he would take and wash for use the things needed for a long trek. There was a wagon he could fix up for the pack horses to pull. Burn everything else, lodges and all. In time there would be nothing left to mark the spot but a few blackened rings on the ground.

"When these two are strong," he told Manuelito,

by way of farewell, "I take them north with me. Far away."

"I go with you," grunted old Manuelito.

A flintiness settled across Sam's face, then was gone. I am setting forth, he mused, to live among my own race. With my Indian family. My half-Arapaho child. My young Arapaho sister. And my brother, drunken old Apache thief and outcast. I cannot forsake them, like a white man. I am weak where I should be iron and iron where I should be forbearing. Like an Indian.

"Yes," he said to them. "We four go together."

THREE

They crossed Red River east of Cache Creek.

Sam cut logs, and he and Manuelito floated the Indian wagon, containing all camp gear and possibles, and hauled it across, swimming their horses. On the north side they dragged on up the bank to dry land, and then they were in the Indian Territory of Oklahoma, five hundred long miles of Texas behind them. There they made camp for the night and started the overdue evening meal. Sam broke out a jug that he had kept hidden from Manuelito. He let it go two rounds, even little Naka being given a diluted sip for the sake of the occasion.

Wicapi took care of the cooking, managing it with the near-noiseless efficiency of a well-trained Arapaho girl. She was never obtrusive at any time. It was she who drove the wagon team, the pair of browns, Naka beside her on the seat, while he rode ahead scouting trail. Manuelito was no hand at all with a team, he soon proved, either whipping the animals to a lather or falling asleep over the lines.

Sam had shortened her name to Capi, he hardly knew why, and taught her to drop his Indian name and call him Sam. She repeated it many times to herself, under her breath, watching his tall figure ahead on the bay horse: "Sam, Sam, Sam . . ." Until she got used to it.

At Llano he had bought from a new merchant shoes and some dress goods for her and Naka. They appeared to be breathlessly grateful for the gifts and packed them safely away in the wagon and went on wearing their beaded moccasins and soft buckskins.

Plenty of food, time, and good care had wrought wonders in them otherwise. They might have been sisters, only a few years difference between them, for they looked somewhat alike, both smooth-skinned with rather small features overshadowed by large, dark eyes that were lustrous and at the same time enigmatic. Both were slim, except that Wicapi—Capi—had filled out, young-womanly. She was an Arapaho maid, wholly conscious of her sex and its eventual fulfillment.

Naka adored her. She was seldom far from her side, seated by her on the wagon, helping her with the camp chores. They slept together in the canvas-topped wagon, and often Sam heard them whispering late in the night. Sam found it difficult to realize that the self-controlled little girl was actually his daughter, that he was her father and his blood ran in her veins. She was unfailingly respectful toward him and so reserved in her demeanor that whenever he heard her giggling with Capi he would pause in what he was doing and look at her in wonder. He was thankful that she had Capi for mother, sister, comrade, relieving him of that impossible role. He would put them both out of his mind and consider the problems of the trail ahead.

For two days after crossing the Red they traveled through dry country without sighting a living soul, but beyond the Little Washita they found water no problem, the creeks being full. When at last they angled onto thc big cattle trail, the Chisholm, Sam once more produced the jug. He let Manuelito get a trifle drunk.

In Sam's opinion there was nothing about an Indian that set him apart from white men in the matter of drinking. He had lived with both. Some Indians who couldn't hold their liquor went on the warpath. He had seen drunken white men go every bit as berserk. So he let Manuelito guzzle a bit and kept an eye on him as he would on any drinking man. Manuelito still wore his hair sort of chopped off scraggly straight and tied with a red rag, as an Apache warrior. And he carried faint tattoo marks on his chin. Well, white men notched their guns, what the hell.

That night, when Capi and Naka had retired into the wagon, Manuelito demanded another go at the jug and Sam finally had to club the old ruffian and take his knife and Winchester from him. Sam then relented a bit. The old boy needed a drink now to pull him together. He started to the wagon for the jug.

The squabble had apparently not disturbed Capi and Naka. As he stepped around the wagon he heard Naka speaking, and he halted. It came to him that he seldom really heard Naka's voice. Most of the time, a self-consciousness kept him and his daughter from exchanging direct speech. When she did speak it was to Capi. The two of them had as little to do as possible with Manuelito, Apache barbarian. Arapahoes and Apaches didn't mix well.

She was speaking in a tone of immense seriousness, a wistful, begging tone, as though in prayer.

". . . I would have little brothers and sisters. I would have father and mother." The child gave the sound of poetry to the long vowels of the Arapaho tongue. "Naka grows lonely for those. *He-ye*! Lonely-lonely-lonely. Her heart is on the ground."

"Sleep," came Capi's voice, gently. "Sleep and dream. Perhaps . . ." Her voice sank to a whisper and ceased.

She suddenly parted thc canvas flaps of the wagon, and there she knelt, gazing out straight into his face. Her small rounded chin trembled. By the light of the campfire Sam saw the hot glow start high on her cheeks. Her large dark eyes, steadying on his, widened for an instant before the lashes half fell, and he could not mistake their eloquence.

Sam clenched fists hard at his sides. He forced forward in his unwilling mind every thought possible of aid in fighting down the swift fire that raced through him. This girl was not simply offering herself to him. She was mutely offering to bear him children, brothers and sisters for Naka.

With great effort and self-control Sam wrenched his gaze from her, and his passion slowly cooled. He would not again take an Indian wife as he had taken Nabilase. He was older now, wiser, and there was no Tall Horse to obey.

The effort he was making set his lean dark face into lines of grim sternness. The lively gleam faded from his eyes, and then something died in hers, too.

"The jug, Capi," he said harshly to her. "Pass the jug out to me, sister." And presently she handed it out to him and silently withdrew, letting the canvas flaps fall together.

Manuelito was sitting up, rubbing his head, scowling ferociously. But he grinned and licked his lips at sight of the jug. Had it been anybody but Sam who clubbed him, he would have set about studying ways and means of evening the score. He got his swig at the jug and, taking advantage of Sam's pondering abstractedness, he sneaked another. He had his flashes of insight, and he growled an earthy brag.

"When I was young—wagh! She would know she had a man!"

Sam, coming to, retrieved the jug. "I am all that you ever were, *bekan-thlaha*, and more," he said dryly.

"Then take her as wife, brother! Take her while the moon is full!"

"No. My woman shall be of my blood. A white woman."

Manuelito wagged his head, deploring opportunities lost. In a moment he asked interestedly, "Are white women, then, made different?"

"Go to bed, you old fool," Sam snapped irritably. "How the blazes would I know?"

At Rush Creek they struck hard luck. Struck it bad. It had rained, and mud and water was belly-deep on the struggling horses. As the wagon pulled out, slithering up the bank, the king-bolt broke. Wagon bed and hind wheels, carrying the camp gear, Capi and Naka and all, rolled back down into the creek.

It took hours to straighten out the mess and get the wagon onto solid ground, by which time Sam was sogged with mud and grease from head to foot. Nor were the others much better off.

So he was not in the best humor for a pleasant parley with the column of cavalrymen that came jogging down the broad trail. Besides, he retained sore recollections of soldiers from the not-too-distant days when to the Plains Indians they were known as the Long Knives and were rounding up the shattered tribes and driving them onto the reservations. Men, women, children, the old, the sick, the pregnant, herded like cattle. That was after the last high tide of Indian resistance, when he was a lad, before the escape with Tall Horse down to Mexico.

In relation to soldiers his mental attitude remained Sioux, and stubbornly recalcitrant Sioux at that. It had not yet struck him that this was an ambiguous attitude on his part inasmuch as he was white.

These wore the insignia of crossed sabers and the numeral 9. Ninth Cavalry, Negro troopers. Big, steady-looking men in dark blue uniforms with brass buttons and a yellow stripe down the leg. Carbines in saddle scabbards. No swords. Warily looking them over, Sam could privately concede that they made an impressive sight. They had an efficient air about them. Their white officer at the head raised a gauntleted hand and the short column came to halt.

Manuelito slung his red roan around to bolt. He had been carrying his Winchester rifle resting across the swell of his saddle, and as he whirled he brought it up, one-hand fashion, its butt sliding snug under his armpit.

Carbines snapped up briskly along the column,

sunlight flashing on clean metal. A command rang out:

"Halt, you, or be dropped!"

A bad opening. The worst. Sighing heavily, Manuelito checked his horse to a standstill and lowered the Winchester. He cut a wicked look at Sam, a look that said plain as day, *This is trouble, brother!*

The white officer, seeing his order obeyed, touched his horse forward. He had an aquiline face, the skin weathered to brown leather, a pointed gray beard, and coldly piercing blue eyes that probed Sam appraisingly.

"This your outfit?" His voice crackled, dry and harsh with accustomed authority.

". . . It is." At once Sam conceived a prickly dislike for the man. His tone, his manner, everything about him rubbed the wrong way.

"Name?"

"Hatch. Yours?"

The officer paused for the space of two breaths. "I'm Colonel Buskirk." A shade elaborately, like one uttering facts already known to everybody, he added, "Out of Fort Reno. On tour of inspection of this district." Then sharply, "What's your business here in the Territory?"

"I'm up from Texas, heading north."

"Your man tried a break. Why?"

"He's Indian." Sam gave it as complete explanation.

"And you?"

"White."

Colonel Buskirk cocked an eyebrow, sweeping a look up and down Sam. He barked, "Sergeant Wells!" A three-striper rode up abreast, snapping formally, "Sir?" and the colonel wagged a gloved forefinger in Sam's direction. "From Texas. Says he's white. What d'you make of him?"

The Negro sergeant scanned Sam seriously. "Could be a boomer, sir. But—" He shook his head slightly.

"Something wrong about him, eh? Got a queer look."

"Yessir. Squaw man, reckon."

"And something else, too, I wager!" Flicking his chill stare over the mud-caked Indian wagon, the colonel paid lingering regard to Capi and Naka sitting bedraggled on the seat. He switched his survey to Manuelito.

"A red roan horse bearing a Running M jaw brand. A single-rig saddle with long scar on left skirt. New Winchester repeater. That say anything to you, Sergeant?"

"Yessir. I read the latest want-lists from Texas. 'Pache killed a white man, took his—"

"Right!" The colonel indicated Capi and Naka with a nod. "Sioux?"

"Arapaho," Sam answered. He felt sorry for Manuelito. If only the crazy old robber had not . . .

"You sure of that?"

His Sioux upbringing had not accustomed Sam to having his word so peremptorily challenged. The officer's brusqueness galled him. He matched curtness to it. "Arapaho, I said."

Sergeant Wells drew his brows together. Colonel Buskirk placed both hands to the small of his back and stretched. He was not at all young, and he possessed the rank to indulge in that telltale gesture of saddle ache. "Their dress looks more Sioux to me," he remarked. "Can you account for it?"

Seething inside, outwardly impassive, Sam shrugged. "What difference? A young woman and a child. They travel with me in peace, doing no wrong. Do they look to you like warriors on the warpath?"

The colonel appeared to cock ears acutely to Sam's manner of speech, and too late Sam realized that he had spoken before thinking and let himself be drawn out.

"They're females," the colonel agreed. "But I think they're Sioux females. Sioux or Arapaho, it's odd they should be coming up from south, from Texas—and from where else? Mexico?"

He shot his narrow head forward. Dropping the mildness that he had allowed to creep into his voice, he spoke with a controlled, biting vehemence.

"There's a strange rumor afloat at Fort Reno,

Hatch—if that's your name. A certain man, known to me, started it going. According to him, the son of Tall Horse has jumped the border. He has come up out of Mexico, where Tall Horse and his recalcitrants have been hiding for years. This son is said to be a medicine man like his father and tough as the devil. He may very likely be making his way northward, probably by this route. Would you know anything about that?"

A coldness hit Sam in the stomach like the thrust of an icicle as the colonel added acid sentence to sentence. He had not dreamed for a moment that the army might entertain a grim interest in him, that soldiers would actually be on the lookout for him.

Yet still he was able to eye the colonel composedly and turn his head in calm deliberateness to Capi and Naka. They sat side by side, immobile, gazing with their most enigmatic eyes at the soldiers. Only he could tell, by their hands, that fear crawled in them. They had picked up some English from him, quite enough to catch the drift. He replied evenly and quietly to the colonel's question.

"I know that these, a young woman and a child, are Arapahoes and nobody's sons."

"Sioux," said the colonel. "And I'm damned interested in any Sioux sign I come upon. Tall Horse carried rare prestige. It's entirely possible the son is bitten by an ambition to fill the old man's place, perhaps even outdo him. All this time in Mexico isn't likely to have tamed him, eh?"

Sam said nothing to that, and the colonel observed reflectively, "We've plenty of malcontents on the reservations, especially among the young bucks. We don't want this fella to get up there among them. He'd stir them up, and the next thing—" He drew a hard breath. "He might even have friends helping him on the way. In my service I've come upon a white renegade or two."

He watched Sam's face as he spoke. Its fixed inexpressiveness placed a restraint upon his discourse, and he couched a command in quiet tones. "Sergeant, search that wagon."

"Yessir."

"Know what you're searching for?"

"Yessir."

Dismounting, the sergeant climbed up into the wagon from the rear, hand on his pistol holster as he ducked under the canvas. In a minute he called, "Some Injun trappings here, sir."

"Women's?"

"Not all, sir. Not these." He reappeared, leaning out from between the canvas flaps. His face wooden, he held up the old painted parfleche for the colonel's inspection. "It's right jam-full of Injun truck, like medicine bags an' I don't know what-all. Knives an'—"

"Indian medicine kit," Sam intoned flatly. A savage humor possessed him to inquire, "Do you have any boils you want lanced, Colonel? Your seat in the saddle seems uneasy, I notice."

A faint anger pulled the colonel's lips straight. He was for a fact recurrently afflicted with incipient boils on the part of anatomy most used by a cavalryman but had thought it to be his own secret cross to bear.

"An' here's this I found under the woman's bed, sir." The sergeant shook out for display a feathered headdress. It was massive, rich in color, a swagger bonnet to which was attached a pair of buffalo horns. Tall Horse had proudly and gravely presented it to Sam on his final initiation as a full-fledged shaman.

Sam checked a start. He had not known that Capi had saved any of his or Tall Horse's formal regalia from the burning of the dead camp. He had left it all behind, keeping only the old parfleche because of its properties. He was bound to it by sworn oath and because it had been handed down to him by Tall Horse.

Colonel Buskirk stared narrow-eyed at the relic of barbaric splendor. "A Sioux medicine man's headdress! First I've seen in quite a while. And that parfleche—it fits the description that we all knew by heart a few years ago. By God! Think of it!"

His chill eyes washed blank with far-off

memories of endless days of forced marches under the desert sun, of successes and failures. And then his voice crashed out in command.

"Sergeant!"

"Sir?"

"Disarm these two men and put them in irons! Corporal Tuttle will take four men and conduct these people as prisoners to Fort Reno."

Sam took slow breath. The colonel, thinking he was preparing to speak, snapped, "You'll have your chance to talk at the fort, when I end tour. Your Apache is a wanted murderer and thief. Your Sioux woman and child belong on the reservation. You are transporting the effects of an outlawed Sioux chief and his son. You say you're white and possibly you may be, but you show some characteristics of a man who has lived too long among Indians. Much too long! You'll have a lot of explaining to do."

Sam twitched a shoulder forward in an Indian shrug. "To what good? Your mind is sealed."

The monosyllabic spareness of the words laid an unexpected strain on the colonel's temper. Sam's unbroken reserve, an unconscious emulation of Tall Horse's immense dignity, notable even among grave Sioux elders, had the power to discompose a man who considered superiority of demeanor his own prerogative. The colonel betrayed his exasperation by the roughness of his reply.

“You and your unwashed Indians will answer my questions when the time comes and answer ’em right, or by God I’ll know the reason why! Corporal Tuttle! Keep them in irons and under close guard until you deliver them at the fort. Inform Captain McNassy that I want them placed in cells, not in the stockade with the boomers.”

FOUR

As prisoners and escort squad proceeded northward game appeared more and more plentiful. Sam noticed much sign of deer, antelope, bear. Wild-turkey flocks sped across meadows. There were beaver and otter in the streams. Good hunting country and finc rich rangc.

And yet, although officially designated as Indian Territory, relatively few Indians roamed into this vast section. The Cherokee Strip lay north. The Iowa and Kickapoo tribes were located east of it. The old Cheyenne and Arapaho stamping grounds were far west.

Cattlemen held leases and permits to use the range for grazing. Homesteading anywhere within its boundaries, however, was forbidden by federal law, the law enforced by army patrols out of Fort Reno. Would-be white settlers—boomers—were out of law. As fast as the army patrols rounded them up and ran them out, though, they slipped back in again. They kept the patrols busy, and some of them were wanted badmen in hiding. . . .

Sam learned this from the casual back-and-forth talk of the four troopers and their corporal. Cowmen hated the boomers, claimed they rustled stock, and whenever they spotted any of them they tipped off their whereabouts to the patrols. At the same time the cowmen themselves bore no love for the army, because the army's job also was to regulate grazing privileges and see to it that no permanent ranches became established in the Territory. The boomers were reputed to have formed a brotherhood for mutual defense, with an organized system of keeping track of soldiers and cowmen and passing the word along by means of spies and scouts.

Listening to the troopers' talk, it struck Sam that these people up here—soldier, cattleman, settler, badman—were all at feuding odds. The only fellow who didn't seem to have his knife out for somebody was the Indian. But the Indian wasn't there, to speak of.

Sam and Manuelito rode their own horses, a watchful trooper alongside each. Disarmed and manacled, Sam held his inner turmoil contained behind a stony mask. But the stoic quality, imposed by self-discipline, was not his by nature. He did not possess the incomplex philosophy of old Manuelito, who, likewise in irons, rode hunched like a dozing crow, indifferent to his fate, since it was taken out of his hands.

Capi drove the wagon, Naka as usual close beside her, and they too appeared dulled to dire circumstance, their eyes blank. The two remaining troopers followed behind. Corporal Tuttle rode in the lead, occasionally paying a glance backward. He was a large young man who wore his hard-earned stripes proudly, showing a pardonable inclination to lord it over the squad. Every time he looked back at his little command the pride was a haughty glow on his solemn black face. A capable man and reliable noncom.

They made halt for the midday meal at a creek near the South Canadian. While Sam and Manuelito stood in manaclcd dctachcdncss Capi prepared food and fire, Naka helping. The soldiers at a separate fire fried their own rations.

Sam had a feeling of being under sharply intent inspection not only by the soldiers but by the eyes of others, unknown and outside of his view. He owned to an acute degree that alert sense, and presently he became aware that Manuelito also felt it. The Apache was peering furtively about from beneath lowered brows, small black eyes raking the distance.

He was not surprised by the thundering arrival of a party of horsemen who descended upon the midday camp as if they owned it and the world.

Their horses all bore the same brand, Circle K, and they were evidently part of a roundup crew. But their eyes, Sam thought, were not the watching eyes that he had felt upon him. These were a tough breed of cowmen, impatient, unlikely to indulge in the precaution of scouting a small camp such as this. Their bleak faces and abrupt manners bespoke anger. Two of them, shirts bloodstained, rode partly supported by others.

The one who obviously held leadership stabbed a forefinger indiscriminately at the wagon and prisoners. Without the courtesy of any preliminary greeting, he demanded, “Are these boomers?”

“We-ell, Mr. Krahn, sort of,” Corporal Tuttle answered him cautiously. “Only sort of.” He had risen to his feet on the arrival of the cowmen, showing more respect to the man he called Mr. Krahn than the man showed to him. The four troopers remained seated at their cookfire, tongues stilled.

Krahn said, “I’ve a mind to let my men take them off your hands!”

Besides the natural bellicosity of a square face, thick neck, and heavy build, he emanated an aura of brute force. His rasping voice matched the hot-tempered arrogance in his eyes. But the clothes he wore set him apart from the average run of cattlemen. He was dressed in a white linen suit, soiled, and a planter’s wide-brimmed Panama hat. The right side of his coat sagged with the weight of a pistol whose handle protruded from his pocket.

The corporal shook his head to the threat. “Not these, Mr. Krahn. No, sir. They got to be delivered at the fort. The colonel’s own orders.”

With a placating reach at humor, he added, "Your men just might misuse their ropes on 'em, Mr. Krahn—"

"There's no *might* about that, the way they feel!" Krahn grated. "Came on some of DeBray's boomers driving off a bunch of my Circle K steers this morning. They took to brush and opened up on us with rifles! Got away!"

"Sorry to hear that, sir."

"Sorry! By God, it's high time the army sent in some *real* troops to clean them out! You buffalo soldiers don't seem able!"

The four seated troopers turned heads slowly to regard one another in wordless eloquence. The corporal's face stiffened. "Us men of the Ninth U. S. Cavalry"—the words were painstakingly distinct—"are doing as good a job as anybody could in the same circumstances, we think . . . sir."

Krahn ignored the polite protest. He swept an angrily contemptuous stare over the camp, taking in details, and settled it on Sam. "A squaw man, h'm? More worthless damn specimens sneaking into this country every day. Outlaws and thieves and bushwhacking boomers—and now this! Find cross-breeding, you find the lowest scum of two races."

"That might be," said the corporal. "The young woman, though, don't seem to be—"

"She's got the marks of a cast-out slut somewhere on her, I'll lay," Krahn interrupted, switching his stare to Capi. She was kneeling at her cookfire, small hands busy, her two thick braids of hair falling forward over her shoulders.

She was making a brave pretense at obliviousness of the cowmen. Beside her, always beside her, Naka sat on her heels, hands in her lap, small image of a woman. Their hands squeezed and shook, while their faces stayed placid, eyes calmly remote from everything but the fire and the cooking.

It must have been the calmness, or the appearance of it, that aroused the ready devil in Krahn. He swung down off his horse, saying, "Some tribes, I've heard, burn a whore brand on them somewhere before they kick them out. Like the scarlet letter. I've never seen it." His square face portrayed two emotions: puritanical intolerance and lewd curiosity. "Let's have a look at you—"

"Mr. Krahn!" Corporal Tuttle cautioned. "I got to tell you not to lay hand on my prisoners."

Disregarding him, Krahn stepped behind Capi, towering over her. "Stand up when a white man speaks to you!" he said, and when she didn't obey him he grabbed one of her braids in his fist and cruelly tugged her up. She whirled swiftly, striking at him.

He used his free hand to cuff her in the face.

Sam leaped, twice, the second leap bringing

him to Krahn. He flung his hands over Krahn's head and slammed the manacles down. Krahn uttered a cry of startled pain and outrage, and Sam hooked the connecting chain under his jaw and into the windpipe. He jerked savagely and brought up his knee. The Circle K owner, throttled and jackknifed, gurgled, sinking, hands clawing at the choking chain.

The group of riders pressed forward instantly, stroking at holsters, and the four troopers jumped to their carbines. Corporal Tuttle's pistol rammed Sam in the ribs.

"Leggo, man—leggo o' him! You're killin' him!"

"I'll kill him, all right!"

"Leggo, man, or I gotta shoot you! Right now!"

Sam let go then, deliberately kneeing Krahn full into the fire, face down. Spilled cookpots and coffee flared and hissed steam. Krahn rolled himself clear, hugging his scorched face in both hands.

Corporal Tuttle, unwittingly lapsing into an early accent, snapped at the Circle K riders, "You shoot, you're shootin' at the Army o' the United States! This man's mah prisoner an' Ah'll defend him till he's delivered to Fort Reno . . . gennlemen!"

They glared, fingering guns, cursing him and the four troopers who stood fast with carbines at the ready. Their boss had suffered a severe mauling. By their code of loyalty it called for blood, and anybody blocking them was on the enemy side. The uniforms of the five cavalrymen alone shielded them from blazing violence.

Two of the furious punchers helped Krahn up onto his legs. He shoved them off with a spreading of arms and mounted his horse unaided. He didn't look as imposing now as formerly, his thick neck and face badly marked and the white linen suit in ruins. Reining his horse half around and motioning departure to his men, he aimed a parting threat at Sam.

"Squaw man, I'll get you for that, believe me—"

When they were gone Corporal Tuttle said very soberly to Sam, "Mr. Krahn is the big smoke in this part of the Territory. Pres'dent of the Pool—the West Oklahoma Cattlemen Pool. His Circle K iron brands cows in the thousands. Mind, I see your side, but you hadn't oughta jumped him, not that hard. Mr. Krahn says he'll get you—he'll *get* you."

"How?" Sam asked. Capi had darted into the wagon with Naka directly after the fracas and not reappeared. Although he was leaning against a wagon wheel he could hear no sound from them. "Will he tell off somebody to do it? A long-range rifle, before we reach the fort?"

The corporal managed a noncommital shrug. "How would I know? You're a fightin' man, I notice. The way you landed on him. Lawdee, if I'd known—! Guess I gotta clamp leg irons on you."

"So I can get killed easier?"

"No. So *you* can't kill *me!*" The corporal walked to his saddlebags to get the leg irons.

Hearing a slight sound, Sam glanced around to see Capi drop lightly to ground from the rear of the wagon. In her hands she gripped a short-barreled pistol, Krahn's black-handled pocket pistol, the hammer cocked. Sam had not seen her filch it out of Krahn's pocket during the fracas, and Krahn evidently had been too roughed-up to notice that he had lost it.

The corporal, at his saddlebags, had his back turned. The four troopers had hunkered down around their fire again, talking in low voices of what had happened and taking care of their cooking.

Capi gave Sam a look of urgent inquiry. She had the gun, but for the moment she didn't know what to say, in English. So Sam, backing to her, said it for her:

"Put up your hands, fellas!"

The corporal spun around, hand slapping holster. The troopers reached for their carbines.

Sam said, "No— You'll be shot dead!"

He fitted his big hand carefully over Capi's small ones, taking the snub-nosed .45 from her. She readily relinquished it. He held it leveled at the corporal, the man he judged most likely to snatch a chance.

"Put up your hands, or I shoot! I shoot fast!" He stared at them, stared them down.

The four troopers put their hands to shoulder level hesitantly. Corporal Tuttle gusted a mighty sigh, raising his, and said growlingly, "Man, you can't do this! It's the army you're pullin' a gun on!"

"Throw me the key to these handcuffs! Be careful!"

The corporal complied, making his movements slow. Capi picked it up off the ground, her movements every bit as slow and wary. She manipulated the key delicately, unfamiliarly, careful not to block the aimed pistol. After a couple of false tries she succeeded in unlocking Sam's handcuffs and then Manuelito's.

"Gather up the guns, Manuelito," Sam told him. "Ours and theirs."

Their weapons had been placed in the corporal's charge. Retrieving the Winchester repeater first, Manuelito evinced an itch to shoot somebody right off by way of celebration. Sam promised to blow his brains out if he did.

"Capi—the wagon. Get started." Breaking out the firing pins of the troopers' carbines, Sam said to Corporal Tuttle, "No following us, you hear? We'll shoot on sight. Sorry, but I don't intend to die in irons."

"You'll be sorrier," the corporal predicted. "Go through with this, every sojer in the Territory will be on the lookout for you. Every cowman. Every fed'ral law officer—"

"I've got to take that chance."

"You'll die a renegade!"

"Not in irons."

Capi slapped the lines on the team, starting them up, and set the wagon rolling, Naka slipping forward onto the seat with her. Sam nodded for Manuelito to follow, but the old Apache delayed, continuing to finger the Winchester.

"I'm leaving you your horses," he told them. "Ride back south. Tell your colonel, when you find him, he's dead wrong about Tall Horse and the son of Tall Horse."

"Right generous of you," muttered the corporal. "He'll bust me for this."

"Sorry," Sam said again. He motioned to Manuelito, and they set out after the wagon.

Catching up on the wagon within a mile, they continued north with it until Sam, scouting ahead, gave signal to quit the trail and angle over eastward after him into country that looked rough enough to suit him. He intended skirting far wide of Fort Reno, avoiding all cow camps, settlements, and horsemen.

The treatment that had been meted out to him and his little Indian caravan rankled. The cold contempt and intolerance. The arrogant insults, suspicion, unjustified violence. A bitter disappointment to a man who had thought of himself as returning at last to his own people. Henceforth, with distrust for all, he would try to stay clear of them and, if he couldn't do that and they crowded him, he would fight them in the brush. He had pushed too far up into this country to cut back now. Alone, he guessed he could elude the cavalry patrols southward. Couldn't do it with the . . . with his family. Only thing left to do was push on, try to get through, out of it.

Then, when he'd got Capi and Naka in the clear, safe some place . . . *then* he would cut back, alone, on the prowl. He was not forgetting the unknown white man who twenty years ago had led the Tonk massacre of his family—his white family—on an unknown creek somewhere in this general region. He was never forgetting that.

Nor a place called, oddly, Desperation; a new range, never reached by his white family. And a name. His family name. His own.

Toward sundown Manuelito showed signs of acute restiveness, turning his head constantly this way and that, black shoe-button eyes glittering, his wrinkled visage screwed in a scowl. He didn't speak of what was itching him, knowing it wasn't necessary. Sam knew his trouble. He had it too, sharper and more imperative now than earlier in the day: the sense of being watched, the awareness of being stalked. His neck hairs tingled.

He held up a hand for Capi to halt the wagon. Manuelito looked at him, then looked away, satisfied that Sam knew what he was doing. Capi, except for a slow glance around, betrayed no uneasiness. As for Naka, only Capi ever knew what thoughts resided in the child's mind.

They went through all the preparations of camping there for the night unhurriedly, giving the impression to any watchers that they felt secure. But after dark they quietly hitched up and struggled on for another hour, finally making camp in a sheltered hollow. The site was a good one, surrounded by low hills and a belt of trees, and a stream ran through it. They built a tiny fire, an Indian fire, bedding it in a scooped-out hole, and ate Capi's cooking.

Afterward Sam packed his pipe and passed his tobacco pouch over to Manuelito. But the tingling sense was coming back, and he stayed his hand from reaching for a light. He met Manuelito's look across the low glow of the fire. It was while Manuelito was making a lengthy to-do of filling the small bowl of his thin-stemmed pipe, stuffing in a shred of tobacco at a time, that a ghostly owl hoot quavered through the hollow.

Manuelito was hunched there by the fire one instant, and the next instant he was gone, slithering as soundlessly out of sight as an alarmed snake. Sam found him crouched behind a tree trunk in the darkness, the Winchester poking motionless from his tattered blanket. They traded brief whispers.

"No owl?"

"No owl! Bad!"

Bad. That could mean anything. An evil spirit on the loose. The ghost of an ancient enemy. A half-crazy brush Apache might go through life discoursing happily with amiable spooks that only he could see, then hear hell coming for him in the noonday croak of a bullfrog.

The call rose once more, this time with an inquiring lift and no flutter: *Ah-hoo-wah*? A travesty of an owl hoot, and not lacking a comic touch. Capi and Naka slipped into the wagon. The tiny cookfire burned low.

Sam felt Manuelito bristling beside him. No Apache could ever hear humor in such a call. A mocking challenge, rather. They were not alone in the hollow, not any longer. Men had crept in, their unseen presence creating a sentient pressure on all sides. His wildness spilling, Manuelito uttered a thin cry.

There was a long silence. Then muffled sounds made themselves heard. Someone walking slowly but without stealth approached the camp. Sam glimpsed the murky figure move forward out from the encircling trees, and he caught the barrel of Manuelito's cocked Winchester and thrust it down. If there had to be shooting he would start it at the critical moment, not at a man obviously advancing to parley. The trees sheltered many other men, waiting, watching, without doubt armed.

The lone man came on close to the dying fire, carrying his hat in his left hand, the right hand raised. He wore a baggy black suit and string tie on a white shirt. His baldhead and pointed beard exaggerated the egg shape of his face.

Sam rose from crouching. He muttered a warning word to Manuelito and walked forward.

“Good evening, Mr. Hatch,” said Dr. Dwyer.

FIVE

The muffled sounds ceased all around the hollow. They started up once more as Dr. Dwyer revived the low fire with a few dry sticks and brought it to blaze. The men among the trees were gradually moving in closer, Sam's ears told him, and he laid a flinty look on the doctor.

"I think," Dwyer said, a trace of discomfort pinching his voice, "you'd better call in your Indian. It wouldn't do for him to fire on the men I'm with."

"Who are they?"

"It wouldn't do," Dwyer repeated. "They're—friends of Boomer DeBray. One of them's hurt. That's why I'm along—"

His strained composure cracked suddenly, and he burst out, "Goddam it, don't stare at me like that! I'm your friend, remember? I invited you north with me. You had something to do first, so I came on."

"You are the 'friend,' I think," Sam said, "who lied about me at Fort Reno. Told them I, as the son of Tall Horse, had crossed the border to stir up the tribes. Friend! You—" His eyes grew bleaker.

"Wait, now! Listen!" Dwyer wiped a hand over his pale brow. "If you're white, act white!

Don't—" Yet Sam had not moved a muscle. Dwyer took hold of himself. "Look, I dropped in at Fort Reno. You know—I was a surgeon with the army once. A few of them there remembered me. They made me welcome, and I got drunk. I talked—when I'm drunk, that drunk, I talk too much."

He spoke jerkily, shamefaced.

"I talked of meeting you. Can't recall all I said—just mouthing off— But I know I couldn't have told 'em you were headed for the warpath. That part's army rumor, nothing but guff that they've tacked on. They were drinking too."

"They believe it. Their colonel put me in irons."

"Let me finish. When I came out of it they were pouring coffee into me. They kept asking me more about you. I wouldn't answer—I'd said too much as it was. There was talk of placing me under arrest, only the surgeon there put me in the infirmary. I had a bad heart, he said. Ignorant fool. Palpitation and the shakes, that's what I had. Alcohol reacts different ways on different people. Like drugs. Although it's anesthetic—"

"I know," Sam broke in. "Go on."

"What? Oh yes. I saw a chance to duck out of the fort and took it. They're looking for me. Those questions, you know, about you . . . your description, so forth. I fell in with DeBray, and he took me to his place. The boomers need a doctor, God knows. Always getting injured. Gunshot wounds mostly." Dwyer paused to listen with Sam to surrounding sounds. "They're moving in. Call off that damned old Indian, will you? Makes me nervous to think he might—"

Sam beckoned to Manuelito. To Dwyer he said, "Your boomer friends have been watching me all day, eh?"

Relieved to divert the subject from his drunken betrayal of Sam, Dwyer relaxed. He hoped Sam would never refer to it again. The steel-blue stare had petrified him for a few bad moments. Damn, could there possibly have been any grain of truth in what those crazy BJ vaqueros . . . ?

He cleared his throat noisily and answered, "From some distance most of the time, with glasses. So you caught on? Well." Instinct, he mused; some men developed the gifts of wild animals. He had none of that himself.

"Yes," he went on, "they saw you slam the great Krahn. A joy to their eyes! Saw you make monkeys of your guards too. Then they had doubts. Your play could've been faked all round. You could be a spy, a plant to lead them into a trap. It's been tried before. I vouched for you, but after all I'm still new here. Some of them are not sure of me yet."

"Cagey," Sam commented, and his recollection harked back to the bandit roosts and thieves' hangouts he had known down along the border country.

"They have to be," Dwyer said. "What swung them over, more or less, was you shifting camp after dark. It showed you didn't want company—theirs or anybody else's. They only found your trail by accident."

"They're an organized gang, are they?" Sam asked.

Not liking that bald term applied to men with whom he had associated himself, Dwyer gave a hasty reply. "Well, they've got to stick together." It was evasive. He attempted to remedy it by adding, "Divided we fall, you know, as DeBray says."

"DeBray," Sam murmured. The name began taking on a vaguely familiar ring to it, the more he heard it spoken. He frowned slightly and shook his head. He had never known anybody by that name.

"DeBray's a cattleman," Dwyer informed him, "but he's on the side of the boomers."

"Why?"

Dwyer's hand went up to stroke his right eyebrow. Somehow it seemed the gesture of a man not too certain of his facts. "For one thing, he's fighting Circle K—" he began, and stopped.

"And uses the boomers against Krahn?"

"It's not only for that. They couldn't do without him. He helps them in every way. DeBray's a good man. He's for the underdog every time. A kind of idealist, if you know what I mean. I guess you do. You're inclined a bit that way yourself, in spite of your—"

Sam said, "Your friends take their time moving in. Why so many of them?"

The little doctor spread his hands, watching Manuelito slink tardily out of the darkness toward them. "A happenstance. I was called out to patch up a man hurt in a scrape with cowmen. We fell in with a party of DeBray's riders sent by him to meet his daughter. She's just returning from a trip to the States."

Capi and Naka just then emerged from the wagon. They figured their place was somewhere near Sam, whoever the callers might be. Dwyer looked a long moment at them, then at Sam. He bobbed his baldhead at them.

"How in hell do you expect to go white, Hatch, saddled with an Indian family?"

"They're the last of my people," Sam said simply. "Could I desert them?"

"I think *I* could. You—no, I suppose not. The last?"

"The rest were all wiped out. Cholera."

"You never should have gone back. Frankly you won't find much respect here for a squaw man. Oh, once in a blue moon you'll meet somebody like DeBray—he preaches equality and so forth as a matter of personal principle. But on the whole—"

"Or like you?"

Dwyer shook his head. "It doesn't matter to me. I don't care enough about anybody. Most of the people here, especially the newcomers, actually know damn little about Indians. They've formed their opinions, though. Or prejudices. To them it's an uprising if some hungry Cherokee steals a cow. A lot of army men aren't much better informed, for that matter. I recall soon after the Custer massacre—"

"Massacre?" Sam snapped him up on it. "Long-hair Custer searched a long way for battle. He found it. He lost."

"Maybe the Indians' trouble is they don't print newspapers," observed Dwyer. "Were you in on the Little Big Horn?"

"No. But by many who were there I heard the—"

"Hearsay! No more reliable than the yellow press. Right and wrong on both sides, as usual. Face the facts, Hatch. If Indians only see the Indian side, don't blame whites for only seeing *their* side. By and large, whites despise Indians. They put them down as sneaking bloodthirsty savages. Custer died a hero and a martyr. Speaking of bloodthirsty savages, your old Apache there is certainly one. His weird howl raised my hair, what there's of it."

"He'd have lifted your hair if I hadn't—"

"I don't doubt that. Most of these people here wouldn't doubt it of any Indian. Here they come,"

Dwyer said hurriedly, lowering his voice. "Don't show surprise at whatever you see and hear. But you won't, of course. Don't even let yourself *feel* surprised. And no temper, mind, for God's sake."

They closed in from all sides to congregate around the camp like a capturing army, some riding at slow walk, some on foot leading their horses. For the most part they were armed with six-shooters in significantly low-slung holsters and rifles in saddle boots—unusual for would-be homesteaders—but here and there a man carried a shotgun in hand.

Sam had never in his life seen boomers, never heard of them before entering the Territory. He unconsciously searched these for some characteristic, some common denominator, as he would have sought marks of tribal identity in a band of strange Indians, friendly or hostile. He failed to discern any. It was an oddly assorted mob, ranging from men who more than matched the tough swagger of Krahn's fighting cowpunchers on down to others in thick-soled boots and overalls.

And then Sam's searching broke off, because a woman rode in through the circle. A young white woman on a dancing all-white mare.

She rode sidesaddle, the first of its kind Sam had seen since he was a small boy, and it gave him a queer shock. It was like a positive sign of assurance that he actually was back among people of his own race. That assurance had somehow been lacking up to now. And she was the first white woman of her kind that he had seen in all those years. He had seen others but none like her.

She wore a long traveling cloak of some silvery gray material that seemed to shimmer as she moved. From beneath the sweeping brim of her feathered hat a thick and shining cascade of hair the color of old gold fell to just below the level of her shoulder. As she firmly reined the white mare out of a spirited curvet her eyes caught the firelight and flashed ice-green. The planes of her face were fine, though having some fullness at cheeks and mouth, especially the mouth. Her skin was not tanned.

Sam could not imagine anything so lovely. She was an explosion of sheer beauty. Her age he had no way of telling. Nineteen or twenty, perhaps. Quite unashamedly he wondered about her body under the covering cloak. Considering her lips, he imagined that it would have the same ripe fullness. Such beauty as hers must carry on through down to her toes.

It did. As if conscious of his speculation and the nature of it, she tossed the cloak back off her shoulders, letting it fall behind her across the cantle of her saddle. The shedding of the cloak revealed, not a heavy riding habit, but a full-skirted green dress.

He raised his eyes and discovered that he was meeting hers. Ice-green. Yes, but not cold. He did not break the look, nor did she. Neither of them was remotely conscious of Capi crouching back into the shadow of the wagon, watching them both frozenly.

Capi had been taught not to hate without good cause. Hatred became self-poison unless you did something about it and so got rid of it. She was trying hard not to hate the dazzlingly beautiful white woman.

Victoria DeBray knew that she was beautiful. She delighted in clothes and hair styles that were out-of-the-ordinary, even daringly flamboyant, for her own satisfaction. The satisfaction never came up to her expectation. There existed in her, she supposed, a streak of chronic discontent. She was twenty-five and had developed a considerable contempt for men, a contempt that guarded her from harmful involvements while adding to her enjoyment of causing them to make fools of themselves.

This tall man with the graven, dark-skinned face. Strange eyes, growing stranger. Almost—Yes, frightening.

She didn't like him. She wrenched her eyes away from his and drew the silvery gray cloak back up over her shoulders and covered herself completely with it up to her chin. Anger chilled her ice-green eyes now, anger at herself as well as at that—that animal. . . .

Her escort, the man who had entered the circle with her, riding closely on her left, took Sam's shift of attention. The man was staring full at him. Beyond question he had witnessed the locked gaze and the woman's byplay with the cloak. And as surely, Sam realized, the man did not intend to tolerate it. Sam studied him.

He was unmistakably in his forties, but he had the springy air and steel-muscled look of an active man half his age. His face, haggardly leonine, contained curious contradictions: the lips down-turned and sardonic, the strong jaw too thrusting, the wide-set eyes pale with the opaque sheen of fresh-cut lead. It was like the face of a fallen angel.

He twitched his big black gelding aside from a wayward plunge of the white mare, and the animal's agonized open mouth displayed broad spade bit and metal burr. A cruel horseman. It was probably the cruelty, Sam thought detachedly, a lifetime of it, that had imposed the inhuman quality on that face.

In a flat voice of authority the man rapped, "What have we got here, boys?"

Nobody replied at once. Dwyer moved toward him, making to speak. The man forestalled him. He wiped a glance over the muddy, battered

Indian wagon, over Capi, Naka, Manuelito and back to Sam. He made answer to his own question, spitting it out in disgust:

"A stinking squaw man!"

Sam sighed deeply, for the moment feeling frustrated and less than himself. In the face of the man's searing antagonism there was little that he could do, hemmed in all around as he was by the pack of riders. Besides, he borc in mind Dwyer's urgent admonition: *No temper, mind, for God's sake!*

Still, it was hard for him to swallow. Not merely the words, acidly biting though they were, but the overbearing animosity. A bad beginning. Damn it, he'd tilted into nothing else than bad beginnings since entering the Territory. Colonel Buskirk of Fort Reno, Krahn of the Circle K—And now this.

Dwyer, moving forward with hands outspread in a gesture of reasonable expostulation, said, "Now wait a minute, Overby, will you please? This is Sam Hatch. He's a wanted man. You weren't with us when we saw what he—"

"Who asked you to pipe up?" Overby's pale eyes dropped to him, the flicker showing again the sheen of cut lead, and pinned the bald-headed little doctor to a standstill.

"I'm only trying to say he's all right." Dwyer was trying more than that, attempting in small measure to make up for the disastrous injury that he had unwittingly done to Sam at Fort Reno. "He's a friend of mine."

"That makes him all right?" Overby asked derisively. "I've got my doubts about you too, sawbones!"

Dwyer appeared to shrink smaller, his courage withering under the blast. Nevertheless he stammered stubbornly on, "That's your p-privilege. To get back to Sam Hatch, here, I can prove—"

"You couldn't prove to me in a thousand years—!"

The girl had averted her face from Sam after pulling on her cloak. She turned now, swiftly and impulsively, and broke in on Overby's caustic declaration. "Let Dr. Dwyer finish speaking, Tobe—if you please!"

As had become his habit when hearing a name, any white man's name, Sam thought: Tobe Overby. Have I ever heard it before? . . . No, never. It rang no bell in his dimmed memories of early boyhood.

Tobe Overby's expression changed subtly, becoming mockingly condescending as he drawled to the girl, "Much as I respect your fine Eastern manners, Victoria, I don't figure etiquette in this case is—"

"If you please!" she repeated firmly, meeting him squarely. For a moment his mocking look held before it faded out, and he clamped his mouth hard shut. “Go on, Doctor.”

Dwyer sent her a look of gratitude. He drew a breath, straightened up, and launched into an account of what he and the party of boomers with him had seen, from Sam’s tangle with Krahn to his escape from the cavalry guards. He was not a good narrator when sober. Being stone-cold sober at present, he made the account as dry and factual as a piece of medical rcporting.

When the doctor had finished Tobe Overby looked slowly around at the gun-slung riders nearest him. “Did you ever,” he inquired evenly, “hear anything like it? This Sam Hatch, this white Indian, this mighty man . . . roughs up Krahn, no less, and sends him and crew tailing off. And he’s in irons, at that. Pulls a gun out of the air then and sticks up the army, gets clean away. My, my!” His tone changed, came as a thin rasp: *“Did you ever hear such hogwash in all your born days?”*

Dwyer backed a step. “But there’s a dozen men here who saw the whole—”

“Shut up!” Overby snarled, so violently that his horse flung up its head. He reined it down savagely. “I don’t care if half the Territory saw it! It’s too much—way too much! It chokes the craw! He’s a plant, your stinking squaw man, this friend of yours! And what does that make you?” He swung to the men he had spoken to. “Shake out your ropes! We’ll soon get the truth of it from 'em! Victoria, you won't want to see this, so—"

"Nobody is going to see it!"

Level-toned as she had spoken, a slight tremble in Victoria DeBray's voice betrayed her apprehension that she was stretching past limits whatever control she had over Tobe Overby. Her face had lost its soft color, and her ice-green eyes showed stark dread that she could not hide. "Nobody!" she said much less levelly.

And yet, on her words, the riders took their hands off their coiled lariats. And sat mute. Seeing that, Tobe Overby rounded on her, his pale eyes wide, almost glaring at her. With visible effort then he wiped off his fury, actually drawing a hand over his face as though arranging a mask. And Sam, holding himself in, hand creeping to gun butt, relaxed a little.

"I thought I was still foreman of Sunrise. I was, the last I talked with your father." Overby spoke in elaborate, rough-edged sarcasm. "Didn't know you were coming home to ramrod the outfit, Victoria. Think you can do it?" The last words were couched as a challenge, still sarcastic, but a definite challenge that bored deeper than the surface meaning.

Perhaps it was the challenge, coupled to discovery of her hold on the men, that restored Victoria's color and the coolness to her eyes. "No, Tobe. You're ramrod of Sunrise—"

"Always!"

"—But your job doesn't include murder. Or torture. I believe Dr. Dwyer." Victoria's voice held not the slightest tremble now. "If he says he saw that man, Hatch, do those things, I believe him. I take him to be a gentleman."

Slightly overcome, Dr. Dwyer bowed to her, hat in hand, and she went on in firm tones:

"As for that man, Hatch, I've neither seen nor heard one scrap of evidence that he's not what Dr. Dwyer says he is."

"And what's that?" asked Overby.

Victoria took a moment to speak, and when she did, it was not in direct reply to the question. She said, "You hold a hard prejudice against him as a squaw man. You actually don't know that he is one." Then to Sam, accompanied by barely a glance to indicate she spoke to him: "Is that young Indian woman your—wife?"

Sam shook his head.

Tobe Overby snorted a harsh laugh. "And that," he drawled, "makes him what? Look at the kid with her!"

Victoria did look. She walked her white mare forward and looked down impersonally at Capi and Naka, both of them trying not to shrink back from this strange white vision with golden hair and green eyes. Victoria reined the mare around and walked it back.

"Only a girl," she said coolly, smoothing her

gloves. "Not nearly old enough to be the mother of that child—a child of that age." She looked at Tobe Overby. "And now I want to get along home. My journey has been rather tiring."

The queenly poise with which she carried that off had its effect on Overby. At first frowning uncertainly after her as she passed by him, he lifted an arm to the surrounding men. "All right, let's go!" he called.

Then in quieter, flat tones: "Bring the mighty man and his Indians along. Can't have him miss out on Sunrise hospitality, so don't take no for an answer, hear?"

Victoria DeBray heard, for she called back, "Oh yes, by all means, Tobe. He's a friend of Dr. Dwyer, so . . ."

SIX

Watching Victoria finish the meal that his housekeeper, Maria, had prepared for her, Colin DeBray felt not at all sure that he was glad to have his daughter back on Sunrise. She would spend the summer here as in past years, and he faced the prospect with mingled feelings of pleasure and dread. He sat across the table from her, hands resting on his knees, the short, thick-set, once-vigorous body absolutely inert, thinking about it.

A strong affection existed between them but comparatively little understanding of each other, especially on his part. He thought back to the laughing blond child who used to scream for him to lean down and haul her up before him onto his saddle. This glossy-haired, utterly beautiful and poised young woman sitting there before him was a stranger. They had been too often and too long apart.

Well, not exactly a stranger. Too much like her mother for that. With a difference, a considerable difference, not in appearance but temperament. Her mother was warm and outgoing, a woman for love. Victoria . . . what had gone wrong with her, anyway? Spoiled, maybe. Everything too easy for her. That summer when she was only fifteen and he owned the only grindstone in these parts . . . young cowpunchers riding in from all over to grind their axes.

The remembrance no longer amused him. His thoughts bent to her mother, his wife. His wife, who had left him long ago. And thinking of her, Colin DeBray murmured unconsciously aloud, "Eugenie . . ."

Victoria gazed at him inquiringly. "What did you say, Father?"

Perhaps she had caught the murmured name. Probably had. Couldn't tell. That beautiful, unreadable face, and those eyes that seemed to look without seeing. "How is your mother?" he asked gruffly.

"She's well. She sends you . . . best wishes."

Best wishes. Humph! And that was that. Victoria's reticence annoyed DeBray. Then privately he had to admit to himself that he was much the same way with her. They had kissed when she arrived an hour ago, had made some attempt to be a bit demonstrative. But even while the men were lugging in her trunks from the spring wagon they had lapsed into desultory talk that told neither of them anything worth knowing. Victoria knew the workings of the ranch and asked intelligent questions which he answered without in turn asking how she spent her time in the East. The East and its doings were foreign to him.

It was very late now. He could hear, outside, some of the men who had ridden in still moving about. Getting settled down, he supposed indifferently. He was taking less and less interest in Sunrise and all that went on, as the years piled up. Ought to get out more, stir around, get things in hand, he guessed. Didn't seem worth the effort.

To break a silence he asked Victoria, "What's this squaw man I heard 'em speak of?"

"Oh . . ." She rose from the table. "A man whose camp we—dropped in on. Friend of Dr. Dwyer. I don't think he's really a squaw man, though. He said not."

"Does it matter?" DeBray sent her a straight look.

She shrugged. "Not to me. Tobe and the rest, though, or most of them— Oh, well." After a pause she said with casual unconcern, "I invited him to Sunrise." Then she called out to the kitchen, "I'm finished, Maria." And to her father: "I think I'll go to bed now. I'm tired out."

He got to his feet and stood while she left the room. It was one of the graces his wife had taught him. Why he continued in them he hardly knew. Victoria warranted the respect, he felt, she being so— Now there, he told himself with tired wryness, was a pretty damn sure sign of how he regarded her. She was a stranger to him. His own daughter. A stranger in the house. And all through this summer . . .

"Good night, Victoria," he called after her. When she was younger he had called her Vic. He waited until he heard her voice in return: "Good night, Father," and he sat heavily down again, blinking slowly.

What, he wondered, had Eugenie told her about him? He had wondered that thousands of times over the years. But Eugenie couldn't have told her about that—that *thing*. If she had, Vic surely would never have come back to Sunrise this summer or any of the previous summers. Besides, Eugenie didn't actually know it herself for certain.

In her room, the door closed, Victoria sat on the bed and gazed unseeingly at the familiar old carpet. "Good night," she whispered, ". . . Dad."

She was shocked and dismayed by the increasing evidence of his disintegration. For almost as far back as she could remember he had been afflicted by some mysterious malady—not a physical ailment, no; like most stockily built men, he had an iron constitution, and his active life outdoors had given him tremendous staying power. It was something else, hidden far down within him, a corrosive disorder of the soul, a sickness of spirit. She attributed it to the breakup of his marriage. He had, she knew, loved Eugenie, her mother, wholly and irrevocably. Still did.

And yet Victoria could never bring herself to blame her mother. Eugenie was above all censure. An Easterner by birth and upbringing, Eugenie had gone back east when she left Sunrise, never to return, taking eight-year-old Victoria with her. Following the subsequent divorce, uncontested by Colin DeBray, she had remarried and been widowed within four years. Left in comfortable circumstances, however, she had been able to give her daughter the advantages of good schools and the sort of background that to some degree she herself had enjoyed. Eugenie had never voiced objection to Victoria spending summers with her father although she invariably gazed at her with an odd kind of troubled expectancy when she returned East.

Why her mother had left and divorced her father, Victoria had no idea. It was a forbidden subject, and she learned never to mention it to either of them.

It must have been an unforgiveable act, she mused now, taking off her shoes and stockings. An act that lay beyond the pale. She did not wish to know what it was.

Then in the middle of a yawn she thought of Sam Hatch. She gulped, instantly angry at him for even intruding into her mind.

"That man!" she whispered, and hurriedly undressing, she got into bed.

• • •

DeBray suspected Tobe Overby of holding vigil at one of the windows, for a minute after Victoria left him the Sunrise ramrod knocked on the door and came on into the house, saying without preamble, "Some of the fellas had another run-in with Circle K, they tell me. Circle K got the worst of it."

DeBray lifted his head and eyed him broodingly. "That's happening too often. Sunrise hands?"

"Boomers." Overby's smoothness of tone made a joke of the term. That same smoothness went into his action as he spun a straight-back chair around and straddled it, both forearms laid across its back, all in a single feline flow of movement.

"Boomers!" DeBray growled. "Not one in five of 'em's a true boomer, and you know it. Hard cases on the make."

Checking the sardonic retort that rose to his lips, Overby realized that the Sunrise owner was in a disturbed mood. Briefly speculating on the reason for it, he laid it to Victoria's arrival. Pretending a genuine puzzlement, however, he asked, "What's eating you, Colin? Sure, they're all hard cases if it comes to that. Isn't that what we wanted?"

"It's what *you* wanted. I went along with it because—" DeBray didn't finish that. He couldn't bring himself to admit that he had lost the will to resist the resolute force of this man Tobe Overby. Presently he burst out with unexpected vehemence, "I don't like it! Damn it, Tobe, we're pushing too far!"

Overby's eyes mirrored a faint, wry amusement as he swung out of his chair and paced to the sideboard where DeBray kept his whisky. He poured a tumbler a third full, took a swallow, and carried the rest of it back to his chair, where he sat steadily regarding DeBray.

"It'll get worse before it gets better," the ramrod said at last. "But when it gets better, Sunrise will be on top—the biggest, richest spread in the Territory. Krahn's grazing permits won't stand up in a federal court, everybody knows. Ours are airtight. Krahn has spread himself out pretty thin, carrying the Pool. He can't stand losses. When Circle K breaks, the Pool breaks. We pick up the pieces. Sunrise is in solid."

DeBray's spurt of energy had already subsided, and he muttered, "Sunrise is big enough for me as it is. What would we do with more?"

"Those are old man's words," Overby commented. "I'm young yet." And then, at DeBray's raised glance, his face chilled, and he said roughly, "I'm young for my years. You're old for yours."

"And so?" DeBray asked. "Look, Tobe, you've had it good here for a long time. You're in as solid as Sunrise. Now you want to risk it on a gamble." He pushed himself onto his feet and strode heavily to the sideboard. "I won't go along with it. I've changed my mind."

Eyeing the broad back of the short man, Tobe Overby let his expression turn saturninely ugly. Instantly he cleared it as DeBray glanced into the mirror above the sideboard. Musingly Overby said, "Those are the exact words you spoke once before, I recall. You were a lot younger then. More flexible, maybe. Anyhow, you finally went along all right—"

He was watching DeBray's square face in the sideboard mirror, watching it with veiled cruelty. The face suddenly sagged. DeBray put down the lifted whisky bottle without pouring a drink from it, his hand shaking. Keeping his back turned to Overby, he said in a strained voice, "We agreed never to bring that up, Tobe—"

"So we did. Just this once I mention it, and no more."

Having delivered the stroke, Overby twisted the knife by saying, "Just this once I mention you've got no more right to Sunrise than I have! I helped you steal it! I did the work! Not you! It wasn't you down on Skeleton Creek that night. Me! With a stinkin' bunch o' drunken Tonks—"

"Shut up! Damn you, shut up!" DeBray was gripping the edge of the sideboard with both hands, his eyes tight-closed, mouthing hoarsely, "Shut up—!"

Overby shrugged. "All right, Colin. Just don't go changing your mind on me that way. I've got my say in this outfit." Bringing the tumbler up, he finished his drink. "Now let's drop it, eh?"

He had DeBray crumpled. It was the first time he'd had to come right out with the thing in twenty years, but he felt that the occasion called for it. Now hc could afford to resume normal relations with DeBray, and he asked casually, "Heard about the squaw man we brought in? Three Indians with him. Squaw, kid, and an old coot that looks to be about a hundred."

DeBray muttered huskily that Victoria had mentioned the man. Trembling, he slopped whisky into a glass and drained it and got back to his chair. Tobe Overby went on talking as if not the slightest thing had gone awry between them. He repeated Dr. Dwyer's account, making it sound completely implausible, and ended with an ominous remark:

"He's a plant, of course. I'll take care of that joker!"

DeBray wearily said, "No, Tobe, lay off. Victoria invited him to Sunrise."

Overby's pale eyes narrowed. "Is that what she said? Well, she . . ." He stopped to reflect that he couldn't very well call Victoria a liar to her father's face. Bad feeling enough for one night.

No point in stirring DeBray up again. And maybe Victoria did think loosely that she had invited Hatch. Maybe.

"I'll see him tomorrow," DeBray said. "Where've you put him up?"

"The doc took him and his Indians along to Despré," Overby answered. "He's a friend of his. I don't like that, not a bit. That joker's a plant, and the doc—"

"Dr. Dwyer," DeBray broke in, "is here by *my* invitation. If the man's a friend of his I want to meet him. Meantime, stay off his neck."

"All right, all *right.*" Overby brought up a grin. "God, you're touchy tonight, Colin." A thought struck him, and he nodded wisely. "Victoria brings your wife to mind, eh? Your wife was a lot of woman. Christ, she could've had any man she wanted! Victoria is a lot of woman too—"

Colin DeBray disliked that turn of talk and, gaining some resurgence of vigor, he said acidly, "Bridle it!"

"Sorry." Overby, rising, set his empty tumbler on the table. "Kind of forgot myself, didn't I? Reason is, I've been fallow too long. And being with her all the way down from—"

"You're old enough to be her father!" DeBray cut him off.

The chill look returned to Overby's face. He hid it from the older man's angry eyes by abruptly pacing to the front door.

"I better catch some sleep. 'Night, Colin."

Outside Overby halted to look all around while he drew several deep breaths of cool night air. Damn, it was a good layout, Sunrise. And he would make it better. The best and biggest. Go on bleeding Circle K, smash it and the Pool, and take over. It would be galling to think that he was doing it for Colin DeBray, for Colin to leave to his daughter.

He was more than foreman of Sunrise. And he would be more yet, much more, in the foreseeable future. His mind, which had not relinquished thoughts of Victoria, turned attention to her. "A lot of woman," he murmured softly.

Old enough to be her father, eh? Well, now . . .

SEVEN

Riding through the straggling street of Despré, the wagon trundling behind and Manuelito bringing up the rear, Dr. Dwyer kept peering aside at Sam in the darkness. He was curious to see Sam register surprise and puzzlement for once, but all he could make out was the glinting shift of Sam's eyes from side to side. He guessed that was about as much as he could hope for from this Indian-raised big moose.

The town could well stir any man to wonder what on earth it was doing there. It stood right slap on Sunrise range, less than a mile from the ranch house. It was not new, and it was anything but impressive; a long scattering of unpainted store buildings, mostly with boarded-up windows, saloons that had gone out of business, and rows of shacks. Only a couple of dim lights showed through cracks, suggesting that the apparently abandoned town still had its uses and maintained forms of life, more or less furtive. There was a feel of alertness about it, like that of an ostensibly deserted Indian camp whose occupants had merely slid into the surrounding brush to watch with faithless eyes the oncoming stranger.

Dwyer chuckled. "Come on, out with it," he

urged Sam. "Ask me anything, I'll tell you what I know."

"This place?"

"Despré. Frenchman built a stage station on the understanding a Kansas-Texas stage line would come through. It didn't. The town took his name. Was a trail town, wild and merry. Then the trail drivers found shorter routes. So you get this. Next question."

"Who lives here?"

". . . Boomers." Dwyer hesitated on the word. "They're sort of transient. Come and go. Soldiers come here looking for 'em, they go. Soldiers go, they come back."

Dwyer was riding a sorrel. He had sold his buckboard and team before quitting Texas and bought the sorrel and a pack horse. In the saddle, wearing plug hat and frock coat and with his pointed beard, he faintly resembled Prince Albert gone to seed. The sorrel had a habit of turning its head to roll an eye back at him.

"That man, the Indian-hater," Sam said. "Overby."

"Sunrise ramrod these many years." Dwyer spoke flatly. "A devil. Just since I've been here he's kicked two men nearly to death for back-talking him. I saw it. Saw his face. He enjoyed it."

"The girl. Victoria DeBray."

"That's a better subject," said Dwyer. He

reached up a hand and stroked his short beard. "I only met her today—that is, yesterday. We got acquainted. Never met as beautiful a woman who could talk as intelligently. We're in her debt for standing up for us against Overby."

"For you. Not for me. She would've let them all take me on until you got yourself mixed in it."

The doctor sent him a solemn side glance. They passed through Despré to the upper end of it. Here the road, such as it was, dwindled to a little-used trail leading toward wooded hills, but Dwyer kept on.

"You know more than the average man, Hatch," he observed then. "A lot of knowledge stored in that noggin of yours, much of it damned queer knowledge." He let a minute pass. The sorrel looked back at him, and he gravely tipped his plug hat and said, as if to the animal, "There's a hell of a lot you don't know. . . ."

A quarter of a mile or so farther along, a huddle of buildings loomed up partly girded by fence posts, the remains of a corral. The doctor drew rein and waved an arm expansively.

"Home, sweet home! This is the old stage station that never saw a stage. I moved in, in the absence of any current incumbent. Dining room and kitchen and two rooms that I take to have been, ah, bedchambers. Barn, harness shed, outhouse . . . all in first-class run-down condition. Welcome, ladies and gentlemen!"

His unusual ebullience—unusual in sobriety—was contagious. Sam caught it and grinned. He heard Capi speaking in a small, almost excited voice to Naka, and suddenly he felt concern for those two tired young females. They had come through it all with him, the long grind up through Texas and his calamities since crossing the Red, doing their part, never a word or look of complaint. He rounded his bay horse to the wagon and spoke to them with an unaccustomed amount of gentleness.

"We stay here for now. Drink a little from the jug and go to your bed. I will take care of the horses."

Capi's eyes glistened in the darkness, and he wondered, uneasily conscience-stricken, if she could actually be crying from fatigue and strained nerves. It hardly seemed possible. Capi, by sheer tenacity the survivor of the Sioux village of death, preserver of little Naka from its horrors, had come through much worse than this without letting down. Nonetheless he felt a sharp pang for her. Naka, worn out and half-asleep, sat resting against Capi.

"Yes . . . Sam." Capi's reply came in a tiny, tight-throated whisper.

"Sleep well, little ones. Have no fear."

"Yes. We have no fear."

What she meant was, she and Naka had no fear as long as he stayed by. Sam sensed that. They felt themselves to be aliens in a strange land of violent, hateful men, hairy white monsters. Arapahoes, as warlike as any when occasion called, were inherently a gentle people, having a high degree of culture, courtesy, morality. They were the creative artists and song makers of the Plains tribes and were said to be the originators of the chastity belt, which Capi assuredly wore beneath her buckskin dress, she being Arapaho and a maid.

Sam said to her, "I shall be close by." And then again, as he reined off: "Sleep well."

They pulled into the yard of the ill-fated old stage station. Dwyer had set up his quarters in what had been the harness shed, because it retained a fairly sound roof, and fixed a pen for his horses. He brought out a lighted lantern while Sam was stripping the wagon team, afterward leading the way to the pen. Capi and Naka crawled back into the wagon to bed. Manuelito sheered off and vanished somewhere on his stolen red roan gelding, stolen Winchester repeater held laid across the swell of the saddle. The old Apache would not trust any place until he had thoroughly scouted it by daylight and assured himself that no evil spirits lurked in dark corners.

After seeing to the horses, Sam looked the place over, Dwyer leading with the lantern. There was a well, but it was clogged, and water had to be carried from a small stream a hundred yards off. The main building, containing kitchen, dining room, and bedrooms, had long been looted of its furnishings. Stars could be seen through the roof. It was shelter, however, the best Sam had known in a long time. He got his bedroll from the wagon—Capi and Naka were already curled asleep together—and carried it in.

Dwyer talked with him while he unstrapped the bedroll and shook it out. "If you stay here any length of time you'll have to take that wagon off and hide it. The soldiers would recognize it if any come snooping up here. Your . . . uh . . . the Indian girls—"

"My daughter and my sister," Sam murmured. "Capi—Wicapi—is the young sister of Nabilase, my wife. Nabilase is dead."

"Sister-in-law," Dwyer corrected him, and to himself pondered on that suffix *in-law.* Indian law? "Tomorrow they better move in with their belongings and yours and set up housekeeping. I think it should be safe enough if they keep out of sight. That is, if you're staying a while, which I hope you will."

Sam said nothing. He was giving it his consideration, and the doctor, mistaking it for reluctance, brought up a couple of clinchers.

"For one thing," Dwyer stated, "you couldn't hope to get out of the Territory now. Not with that rig and looking as you are. They'll be on the watch for you. Soldiers and federal law officers. They've got the telegraph, if you know what that is. And then the cowmen of the Pool— You can bet Krahn is spreading the word, after what you did to him.

"And for another thing," he went on, giving Sam no chance to comment, "your horses are pretty well lanked down. They need to rest and fill out, or you'll be afoot."

Sam had the same thought, and he nodded. "Tomorrow—I mean today, when it's light—I'll unload the wagon and hide it."

"Change your clothes too, if you've got others to wear," Dwyer told him. "They're noticeable. So's your hair. Needs cutting. I'll do that for you. And shave."

"I'll do that."

"Good. Sunrise maintains a commissary, so there's no trouble about buying supplies here. Can get grain too. Well, I'll let you turn in. Need I say I'm glad to have you here, Hatch?"

"Thanks. One last question. Why is Sunrise fighting Circle K, d'you know?"

Dwyer lifted the lighted lantern and turned down the wick. He took time doing it and finally replied, "As I hear it told, it started as a personal thing on Krahn's part. Last summer, they say, he thought he was making time with Victoria. Seems he cuts a dash when he's slicked up. She made a prize fool of him," he ended sparely, "and Krahn's not a forgiving kind of man. Good night."

So it was that Sam carried Capi's and Naka's bed and scanty belongings into the larger of the two bedrooms next morning, himself taking the smaller one. He didn't have to warn them to keep an eye out for any soldiers who might happen along this way. They would do that, all right. "Poor kids," he thought, the pang of conscience again pricking him.

It probably was wrong to have brought them here into these surroundings that were more foreign to them, and less kindly, than had existed below the Mexican border, where isolation had at least protected them from exposure to hostile contempt. There had been no alternative and no means of reckoning on what awaited him and them here in the Territory. Still, it was all wrong for them, a couple of homeless waifs clinging together for comfort, utterly dependent upon him—a hunted man.

What Capi and Naka thought of the move in under a strange roof, they didn't say. They set about cleaning up the place, which needed it. There was a rock chimney in the back wall of the kitchen, made to accommodate the flue of a missing cookstove, and by knocking out a few of the lower rocks Sam contrived a kind of raised open fireplace for Capi to do her cooking.

Sam then hitched up the team and took the empty wagon off, first removing its canvas top. Following a dry creek bed up until he came to a spot where it bent and widened, flanked by high banks, he left it there and took the team back. He then bathed in the stream, shaved in the kitchen, and changed clothes in his bedroom, donning clean Levi's and flannel shirt.

"Goddam, you look human now," Dwyer commented when Sam walked out into the yard. "Let's get at cutting your hair."

All this wrought sufficient change in Sam's appearance that a Sunrise man who rode up failed to know him at first. The man had been one of Tobe Overby's group last night, and he called out to Sam in the yard, "Where's Hatch?"

"Me," Sam said.

The man squinted the sun from his eyes. "Sure . . . I see now. DeBray wants you up at the house. Don't keep him waitin'!"

"Sharp order," Sam observed to Dwyer, as the rider wheeled at once and loped back the way he had come. "I could've told that fella, if he'd waited for it, to tell DeBray to go to hell."

"They get that from Overby," Dwyer said, "not from DeBray. He's all right. Not too hard to get along with. Don't tell him to go to hell, though. DeBray is Sunrise, and Sunrise is the living world around here. I'd mosey up and see him if I were you. Throw the chip off."

With a faint grin Sam raised a hand and brushed his shoulder and went to saddle the bay.

Although the ranch house itself was not overly large nor pretentious, by daylight the Sunrise layout could be seen for what it was, a sizable outfit employing a considerable crew of men. It had two bunkhouses, the cookshack between them, and there was a smaller house that Sam took to be the ranch foreman's own private quarters; a rare privilege that signified the standing here of Tobe Overby.

Bearing out Sam's surmise, the ramrod emerged from that house as Sam rode up from the open gate. Overby's sweeping glance fastened on him at once, and for an instant he paused in mid-stride, seeming to contemplate stalking to meet him. Sam tightened up in certainty that he and Overby were to have it out, now or later. He was ready for the clash any time.

Abruptly then, the ramrod changed course, calling out to somebody beyond Sam's range of view, something about a horse. Sam, letting his muscles slacken, jogged on to the main house. Overby would, he guessed, pick his own best time. He speculated on the reason for the man's enmity and found it in himself. A mutual and instantaneous antipathy. And triggered, of course, by the manner in which he had looked at Victoria DeBray, and she at him.

Well—Sam twitched his lower lip in an unamused smile—Overby was wrong if he thought Victoria DeBray's look at him, Sam, had meant anything remotely promising. Dead wrong. She had plainly evinced an aversion to him.

In front of the house a cowpuncher was minutely examining the feet of a saddled black-and-white pinto pony, a flashy animal but of fine conformation. The saddle was black, ornamented with silver conchas. A pretty fancy turnout. The cowpuncher laid a look on Sam drawing up and lowered his head again. Sam tied the bay to a porch rail, seeing by the worn signs that that was the custom, and mounted onto the low porch.

The front door stood wide open. He was raising his knuckles to rap the doorframe when a voice within bade him enter, and he stepped from blazing sunshine into relative coolness of the shaded interior. The owner of the voice did not speak again, nor did Sam locate him at once, the transition from light to shade placing him at a disadvantage.

Restoring eyesight informed him that the living room he stood in was as unpretentious as the outside of the house. The furniture was comfortable and ordinary, a bit shabby, like an ordinary man's favorite old coat. The carpet was worn in paths showing that the center table and other heavy pieces occupied unaltered positions, another indication that this was a man's house and that the man had settled into fixed habits.

And now he saw the man who had bidden him to come on in, and he stood startled.

The man was short and thickset. He had a square face and a rough thatch of white hair. He sat in an armchair, thick fingers gripping the arms, not moving a muscle. His face was gray, the lips bloodless and stretched tight in a fixed grimace resembling the death grin, and he seemed not to be breathing. He was staring at Sam, staring wildly, as if seeing someone or something entirely different.

"Anything wrong?" Sam asked him quickly. "Should I call—?"

"No!" The word came in a gasp. Slowly the man came out of it, moved his hands, began breathing stertorously. "Nothing wrong—at all—Why should there be?" After two false tries he pushed himself shakily up onto his feet and trod, swaying, to the sideboard, repeating, "Why should there be? Nothing—"

He fumbled for a glass, knocked it over. Letting it roll off down onto the carpet, he drank from the bottle. The sounds of his swallowing were loud. He coughed, bowing his head and sputtering whisky all over the sideboard. The spasm over, he asked Sam belatedly, "Drink?"

and the tilt of head suggested an acute listening for the reply.

"No thanks." The man had, Sam supposed, suffered some kind of attack, and vanity would not let him admit it.

"I'm—" The man kept his back turned to Sam and spoke with difficulty, "My name is DeBray." The impression of acute listening intensified.

"Hatch," Sam said. "Sam Hatch."

"Sam . . . Hatch?" DeBray was having tremendous trouble pulling himself together. He could not control his hands or his breathing. A look into the sideboard mirror showed his face ravaged and ghastly. He'd had the shock of his life when Sam walked in.

Hatch, he thought now; Hatch. Where—? "Oh yes," he said. "Yes, of course—" He drank more from the bottle, put the bottle back, and forced himself to turn around. "Dr. Dwyer spoke of you. You're the reason he's dodging the soldiers."

"He's the reason *I'm* dodging the soldiers," Sam said.

"Yeah." DeBray made it back to his armchair and sank into it, nodding his head in an abstracted way. "Yeah, yeah. He got on a drunk at Fort Reno and let his tongue loose . . . and Fort Reno is after him to loosen it some more. Yeah." The whisky he had gulped was beginning its effect, quelling his screaming nerves, bringing color back to his face. Long time since he'd had to use the bottle for a crutch. He thought once more: Hatch, take it easy. . . .

He had been too shattered to think of asking Sam to sit down, and now he motioned at a chair. A door was opening as he was saying, "The doctor has been drunk again since, here, and talked to me. You're the squaw man, one they call Shaman Sam—" Then his daughter was in the room, and he heaved to his feet, trying desperately to act and appear normal in her eyes.

EIGHT

Today Victoria was dressed for riding stride-saddle, not a sidesaddle. And, typically, her garb was out of the ordinary, at least for these parts. She wore white whipcord breeches and white silk shirt open at the neck, and for contrast her belt and English riding boots were black. In place of a hat she had tied on a black-and-white kerchief, aslant and pirate-fashion, knotted at the back and the long ends flowing free. From beneath it her glossy old-gold hair swept to her shoulders in a single wave.

Colin DeBray need not have worried that his daughter would detect anything amiss in him. She stopped short upon entering the living room, her gaze directly on Sam. Her ice-green eyes flared at their corners, then the lids and lashes lowered slightly, and a trace of flush rose in her cheeks as she sent him a nod.

"This is—" DeBray began. "Oh, you met. Last night. I forgot." According to Victoria, it was she who had invited this man to Sunrise, this dark-faced man calling himself Sam Hatch. And that was the essence of irony. DeBray choked down a mad impulse to laugh aloud. His own daughter—!

"Yes," Victoria acknowledged, hardly knowing what else to say. The sudden sight of the tall, grave, clean-shaven man had thrown her off balance, and she was inwardly fighting to preserve her poise. He was the same size and the same build, and his eyes were the same blue-steel and to her strangely magnetic. In other respects he was not the raw, half-savage animal in mud-caked rags of last night, mutely daring Tobe Overby and the whole crowd to come at him. His appearance was changed. He was a very clean-looking, self-possessed man whose presence filled the room.

He nodded his dark head to her, saying nothing. Because it angered her that he should have that effect upon her she was prodded into rashly taking the offensive in an effort to destroy his composure.

She turned to her father and asked, "As I came in—what were you saying Mr. Hatch was called? Shaman?" Then with a glinting look at Sam: "Doesn't that mean an Indian witch doctor?"

Sam had believed the name Shaman Sam left forever behind down on the border. Dr. Dwyer in his drinking spells was a dangerous friend to have.

He said quietly, "I was a medicine man of the Sioux."

It took her aback. "But how could that be? Or are you a half-breed?"

"I'm white," he said. "I was taken as a boy . . . and later adopted into a tribe of the Oglala." He smiled at her, the smile cold and containing not a shred of amusement. "I was a white Indian for fourteen years. It was kind of them to . . . accept me. I have not met such kindness since."

She crimsoned as his precise words bit in, horribly ashamed, aware that he was holding in leash an anger of his own. Wishing to unearth some way to make amends, to let him know that she was not cruelly unkind, she stammered, "You were—taken as a boy? Taken captive? Your family—?"

"Massacred," he told her in a tone that he made matter-of-fact. And Colin DeBray, leaning intently forward for that reply, sank back into his armchair and released a shuddering sigh. "On a creek," Sam said, "somewhere near Red River, I think. By some tramp Tonkawas led by—" Discretion then closed his mouth.

She dared to say, "You speak well, considering most of your life has been spent among Indians."

He sensed her desire now to rectify her previous tartness, and his smile warmed as he said, "I was seven years old when I was taken. I could read and write—my mother saw to that. And for six years I've been on my own." He added reminiscently, "I've read everything I could lay hands on. Arbuckle's used to give away books with every twenty-five pounds of coffee. I've come on those books in the durnedest places.

There was one I remember called *Romeo and Juliet*—"

" 'Which are the children of an idle brain—' " she said.

" 'Begot of nothing but vain fantasy,' " he finished for her.

She smiled dazzlingly at him, knowing with an immense relief that she was forgiven. "You have an excellent memory!"

"Indian training," he murmured. "Indians have no written language. They have to memorize everything; their history, religion, songs, everything. As a medicine man it was one of my duties to remember."

"A human encyclopedia?"

He had to think hard to catch her meaning. When he did catch it he shook his head. "No. The living present—what I've learned personally—is as much as I can handle. The Sioux memory goes back centuries. I've met Sioux, old ones, who spoke of red-bearded men, blue-eyed Vikings, Danes, who long ago trekked 'cross-country and became swallowed in the tribes of Sioux and Cheyenne and Arapaho. To this day you'll find blue-eyed ones in the tribes of the plains. Like me. My eyes gained me acceptance among the Sioux. I was one of them."

He had talked much longer than was usual for him. His eyes, Victoria thought, looking into them and transfixed by them, were the most striking thing about him despite his large size and his overwhelming personality. He was very much a man, his maleness so strong to the senses that she felt as though she had never met a man before.

All at once she didn't want her father's dour presence, and she asked rather breathlessly and without any forethought, "You're staying with Dr. Dwyer? I'll ride back with you. I—I want a talk with him—" And blushed hotly after she said it, as though she had said something incriminating and less than ladylike.

Sam said to her, his spirits soaring, his dark face a grave mask, "I'd be glad of your company . . . Miss DeBray."

"Victoria," she said, while part of her mind stood aghast at herself. Helplessly she appended, "Dad used to call me Vic. And sometimes Vicky."

The whole wide world opening up before him, Sam could only find it in himself to say sparely, "Glad—" and for once in his life felt stupid. "I'm called Sam."

Her mental and emotional balance partly restored by an exertion of will, Victoria drew on her gloves, saying, "Shall we go, Sam? Oh, excuse me, Father—had you finished speaking?"

Sunk in his chair, Colin DeBray nodded wordlessly. Victoria then perceived the deep-lined grayness of his features, the glassy stare of his eyes, and her lips parted. Yet she could pass no remark to him about it. Any expressed concern, even during his worst spells, had always aroused a thorny irascibility in her father. So she walked to the open door, Sam behind her.

At the door Sam remembered to turn and say, “Glad to have met you, sir.” An inexplicable look was in the older man’s eyes, of abysmal dismay, before they were lowered.

Unable to trust himself to speak, DeBray watched his daughter and Sam leave together. He had not failed to heed the singular effect of Sam’s presence upon Victoria, her high color and her restrained animation. In his head a voice groaned, *Oh, God, no! Don’t let it be!*

Outside in front of the house, the cowpuncher who had been examining the feet of the black-and-white pinto was no longer there. In his place Tobe Overby stood waiting, holding the reins of the pinto and, with harder grip, the bridle of a tall sorrel horse.

Skimming the merest glance at Sam, Overby tipped his hat to Victoria and asked her perfunctorily, “Ready to ride?”

Whether there was previous understanding that Overby was to accompany Victoria on her ride, Sam didn’t know. If so, it could not have been definite, he guessed, because she replied in some uncertainty, “Yes, Tobe—with Sam . . . Hatch.”

Her words could have shaped the blackest of insults, for the instant reaction they produced on the Sunrise ramrod. A spasm of killing rage washed over his gaunt face. His free right hand shifted, barely perceptibly, his chill glare switching to Sam. Sam watched that hand, prepared to match its further motion. Tobe Overby saw that and, studying this man at close quarters, sensed the swift tension and readiness of one who might well be equipped to hand out more than he received.

Victoria, paling, said, "I'm going with him because I want to see Dr. Dwyer," and that broke the deadlock.

Overby stepped away from the horses. He kept his eyes on Sam while drawling to Victoria, "Give the doc my regards . . . and don't let this half-breed lift your hair!"

Sam shrugged, deciding to overlook the slur. Victoria quickly mounted the pinto and reined away from the house, and Sam followed on the big bay. They came abreast and jogged off down to the high-arched gate of the ranchyard.

For a minute Tobe Overby followed them with his narrow stare. He uttered a harsh grunt, swung violently around, and stalked into the house.

"Hell's fire!" he burst out, entering the living room. The frayed edge of a Navajo rug dragged his spurred heel, and viciously he kicked it all rumpled aside. "You flag me away from her! You jerk up on me if I so much as drop a man's remark about her! By God—!"

DeBray, remaining sunk motionless in his armchair, lifted somber eyes to the ramrod. "Don't you march in here using that tone to me, Tobe! Don't push me too far!"

"You sit there like—"

"Snub it!"

A wicked glint was lighting up in DeBray's eyes. Overby saw it and was nevertheless in too gnashing a rage to care as he slammed his hand down flat on the table. "By God, I'm not good enough, yet you let her go riding off with that half-breed!"

DeBray regarded him sharply, suddenly attentive to the words rather than to tone and manner. So, he thought, it's gone that far with him, has it? Should have expected it. Got to handle this damned cagey. . . .

Aloud he said, "There's no bridle on my daughter. She's of age and her own boss. And that fella isn't any half-breed. I can tell you who he is."

Overby, his hand cutting the air impatiently, began, "I don't give a damn in hell who—"

"You better give a damn," DeBray interrupted him. "In hell or out."

"What are you driving at, Colin?"

"That's better," DeBray said. "Sit down." He

too now spoke very quietly. "You didn't get much of a look at the man you killed on Skeleton Creek, did you?"

"John Heward?" Overby murmured the name callously. "No. Knew it was him by the Half-moon brand on his wagon, his time of travel, everything. Why?"

DeBray moved in the chair, planting both feet on the floor, hands on his knees. "When I hired to shift Heward's outfit I lived with him while he checked up on my letters of recommend and my back history in general. The letters were genuine. My history was clean. I was honest at that time—"

Overby wagged his head. "Get back to this Hatch."

"I'm doing that," DeBray said. "He's the spitting image of John Heward!"

The ramrod eyed him curiously. "What are you saying? That's plain impossible."

"Is it? Why wouldn't he be? John Heward was his father. Think back. The boy's body wasn't found with the others, remember."

Overby had not sat down. He did now, leaning forward, one elbow on the table and fingers working at his lips. "How that happened I'll never know," he admitted reflectively. "Figured the kid had crawled off and died and the coyotes got his bones. But you can't be sure of this—"

"I'm sure." DeBray nodded slowly. "Dead

positive. He tells the story. I sat here and listened to him. He got picked up by some Indians and raised as one."

"The hell!" Overby whispered. "Does he know his name and all?"

"He was seven and could read and write. You can lay a bet he remembers it. How much else, who can tell? That face of his! My name didn't seem to mean anything special to him. The boy didn't hear it spoken much. And I've changed. But there again—"

"And he's using a wrong name," said Overby. "And from his looks he's knocked around in some funny places. Huh!" After a moment of meditative silence between the two men their eyes met, and Overby murmured, "That white Indian is on the long hunt!"

"For us!"

"Natchally."

Rising and going to the sideboard, Overby poured two drinks which he brought back, handing one to DeBray. He said in the nature of a toast, "We're in it together—then, now, and all the way!" They drank, and he appended, "We'll cook that duck!"

DeBray shook his head. "There'll be no bushwhack job done while Victoria is here! I won't have it! He probably doesn't have any suspicion who we are. Leave him be, and in a few days he'll drift on out of the country."

"S'pose he doesn't? S'pose he stumbles on something that pricks up his ears?"

"There's nothing he can stumble on, Tobe. Anyway, he's a badly wanted fugitive. The soldiers will catch up with him, and that's the end of it."

"Colin, you're not using your head!" Overby stated. "He'd be bound to tell his story at Fort Reno. Then what? We don't know how much he knows. The Skeleton Creek job's not forgotten. A while ago you told me to think back. Now I'm telling you—"

"I don't want to—"

"Listen, damn it! The Tonks burned the wagon and the bodies. No identification. But this joker knows who they were! S'pose the army and the law got interested in his story and began tracing back? John Heward's outfit, the Halfmoon, started for new location and arrived here as the Sunrise outfit, owned by Colin DeBray! Don't forget it was the crew I got you that did the brand changing. We've kept the brand ever since—properly registered too, by God!"

"I'm not likely ever to forget it," DeBray growled, "having you to remind me."

"Any smart lawman could trace the thing," Overby went on relentlessly, "once he got to figuring it through. John Heward heads north to his outfit, and he don't reach it. It was him and his family got jumped at Skeleton Creek—this joker knows that, mind, and that's the key to the whole thing! I don't say it could be proved after all this time, but you'd sure have some talking to do, Colin!"

"And you, Tobe!"

"If," said Overby, "this Hatch gave us time to talk. Which he wouldn't. I peg him for a fast hard case. A bad white Indian. So I say we make a good Indian of him, damn quick!"

"No," DeBray reiterated. "No bushwhack on Sunrise. Not with Victoria here. . . ." Then aware of the ramrod's stiffening resoluteness, "If there is . . . I warn you, Tobe, if there is I'll go to Fort Reno myself!"

"Careful, Colin! Careful!"

"Me? No, you! I'd lose Sunrise. I'd end in jail. You'd lose your life at the end of a rope!"

A shiver of fury swept through Overby. He eyed DeBray, trying to measure his unusual determination and to find the reason behind his deadly threat.

"This is a new tack for you," he murmured. "I'm wondering if you've got something up your sleeve. I just wonder—" But the next instant caution dictated that he turn on a rueful smile, and with it he said, "We're fools to quarrel. Too much to lose. I'll get on over to the east draws, see how the work's going there."

Riding out from the Sunrise layout, Overby broke the dam of his wrath with a fit of cursing.

Presently he brought his seething thoughts to work. Colin DeBray, ordinarily uninterested and moody, had suddenly and unaccountably become dangerous. It genuinely puzzled Overby.

"Don't force his hand," he muttered to himself. "It's too soon."

His plans for his own future, he decided, would have to be put into operation pretty quick now. It was sooner than he had intended. He had counted on having the whole summer to put them through, but DeBray's attitude—and Victoria's, too, come to that . . .

The man who called himself Hatch, though, came first. Hatch had to be taken care of right away. He was too dangerous to live.

Overby continued on east at his steady gait until over the nearest rise. There he swung northward on a circling course that would bring him into the semideserted old trail town of Despré.

NINE

They had passed through Despré and were walking their horses the short distance farther on to the one-time stage station when Victoria felt required to mention Tobe Overby. She had not, she told Sam, given Overby any reason to believe that she would ride with him today; therefore his anger was hardly justified.

"He's got a sweet disposition," Sam commented.

The dryness of that remark was not lost on Victoria, who said soberly, "He's a man to be feared. He *is* feared, I know. At times I think even my father fears him."

"Do you?"

Not meeting that blunt question immediately, she said, "Tobe runs Sunrise pretty much in his own way. He does as he pleases. Walks into the house at any time. Makes free with my father's whisky, anything. I know that the Western ways aren't like the ways back East. I was born here. But Tobe's manner is insolent, not free and easy. And my father does nothing to check him."

She turned her face to Sam and away again, quickly, as though to prevent him from discerning too much. "Yes . . . under certain circumstances . . . I would be afraid of Tobe Overby! In past years I always found it hard to stand him. I tried not to show it. This year it seems . . . harder."

"Your father owns Sunrise," Sam reminded her, frowning. "He could fire Overby any time. And I suppose some day you'll inherit the outfit, so—"

"I can't imagine his taking orders from me. When that day comes I shall sell out Sunrise." Victoria pushed the kerchief farther back off her forehead. The afternoon was hot. "I hope that won't be for a long time yet, but I feel that it may. My father is aging fast before his time."

"Seems a pity to sell a fine outfit," Sam observed. "The location is good."

"Yes, but Sunrise doesn't own it," she explained. "Only the stock and equipment. The land is all under lease and permit, and a government order now forbids the erecting of permanent buildings and fences in the Territory. Ours were built before the order went in. Circle K, for instance, has to make do with temporary cabins and tent shacks. It's a cause of bad feeling, and I wouldn't be terribly surprised if one day the army ordered us to tear down our buildings. So you see, Sunrise isn't as permanent as it seems. It just happens to have been here the longest."

They were coming up to the stage station now, and on close approach they heard from inside some quiet sounds of busy activity and young feminine laughter. Victoria, all at once self-conscious, glanced fleetingly aside at Sam's face and saw only thoughtfulness. She did not know what his relationship to Capi and Naka was, except that he had said Capi was not his wife. She wished she could think of a tactful way of asking him. It was so outrageously odd, although he apparently gave it no thought, that he should have a young Indian woman and a little girl camping along under his wing. Victoria used the word *odd* in her mind, unwilling to use a stronger one.

It was a happy sound, a heart-lifting sound. The laughter of Indian girls had never failed to delight Sam and raise his spirits. They laughed with such joyousness. Those two in there were enjoying a private joke—a droll remark, a merry accident, a slip of the tongue, something comical . . .

The laughter went mute as Victoria and Sam arrived outside. It was cut off, and there was no more of it. Victoria had begun to smile, caught almost against her will by the infection of merriment. When it ceased so suddenly, she flinched slightly, as if from a slap in the face. She did not know, Sam supposed, that Indian girls were shy and fell silent at the approach of a stranger.

Manuelito squatted brooding on the ground in the shade of the station. Sam knew exactly what he was brooding over. The jug. He had securely hidden it. Manuelito hadn't found it yet and was condemning Sam as a false brother and an ungenerous son of seventeen devils. He wouldn't even raise his eyes. Victoria's pretty pinto danced delicately away from the scowling old Apache, without hindrance from Victoria.

Dr. Dwyer came to the door of his quarters in the harness shed and, expressing not the slightest surprise, he greeted Victoria courteously and a shade pompously. "Welcome, Miss DeBray, to our establishment. I trust you are rested from your journey."

"Thank you, Doctor." Victoria dismounted. "I wanted to see you—"

"Professionally, Miss DeBray?"

"Well, yes. I'm—"

"You look well. Very well indeed, if I may say so," stated Dwyer, which gave Sam a suspicion that he had been drinking. "Your esteemed visit, then, is not occasioned by any upset in your own condition."

"No. It's—"

"Then it must be your esteemed father."

"It is."

"Ah!" exclaimed Dwyer triumphantly, and Sam wondered then how much he had drunk and where he had got it from.

"I'm worried about my father," Victoria said hurriedly before the doctor could break in again. "He's not at all well. You must have seen it for yourself."

The doctor was one man out of Texas who did

not wear his hat indoors, and his immense bald pate shone as he bobbed it up and down several times. "Not a well man. Not well at all, your esteemed father." He blinked reflectively. "Not long ago he let me look him over. Couldn't find anything in particular wrong with him. Low vitality— But say! You've got a medicine man right with you! First rate! Should've consulted him."

"I didn't think of it," Victoria said seriously.

Dwyer chuckled. "My little joke." And a hell of a time for it, Sam thought. "No, Miss DeBray"—Dwyer wiped off his smile—"he's not well. Very low vitality."

"Last night," she told him, "it was very late when he went to bed. Yet I could hear him moving about long afterward. This morning he admitted to me that he's not sleeping well. Could that be the cause?"

Dwyer rubbed his nose with a forefinger, pondering, "I'll give him something for that. You can take it back with you. A spoonful at night, and he'll sleep." He withdrew into the harness shed, and Victoria sent Sam a somewhat helpless glance.

"It may be what your father needs," Sam said to her.

Dwyer promptly poked his head out the door to nod it at Sam. "There's a living sleep maker! Does it with incantations and hypnotism and a few herbs . . . Do anything with 'em! Turn himself into a black wolf! Cut your leg off, and you don't feel it! Anything you like—!" Venting his chuckle mockingly, he pulled his head back in.

Sam could have wrung Dwyer's neck. Drinking loosened the little doctor's tongue entirely too much. The hell of it was, he mixed enough fact with fancy to make it sound plausible. It wasn't any wonder that he had got Fort Reno all stirred up looking for an Oglala shaman-warrior at large to raise war.

The stage station stayed hushed.

In Despré the only saloon was Ves Whiteside's ill-named Lucky Jack. Caught in the town's decay, the Lucky Jack had lost all its ornate garnish, and Whiteside had done nothing to restore it since he moved in.

Only the frame of the back-bar mirror remained, looters having carted off the mirror, along with brass bar fittings and anything else movable. Only the heavy mahogany bar remained, bullet-blemished and never cleaned. Whiteside sold whisky cut with homemade alcohol, by drink or bottle, and his kind of trade wasn't particular about cleanliness.

Tobe Overby, who had been toying with his glass until a couple of boomers departed leaving him as lone customer, now sipped from it and pulled a face. "I've tasted Indian-trade whisky that was better'n this stuff," he observed to Whiteside, who leaned opposite him on the inside edge of the bar.

"Throw it on the floor then."

"It'd rot a hole."

Whiteside only shrugged. He was a bloated, unhealthy man whose eyes were sour slits behind the puffiness of discolored lids. The town suit and yellow vest that he wore at all times were seedy and stained, and the brim of his black derby was greasy from fingering. For reasons of his own he kept himself under cover, living on the premises, with a sharp eye for federal law officers. Although tolerated by Overby, he was not under Sunrise protection as were the boomers and others.

Out of a clear sky Overby now asked him, "Have you still got the clothes that belonged to those two army deserters you staked?"

A thin smile lifted the corners of Whiteside's mouth. The saloon man had known, as soon as the Sunrise ramrod entered, that he wanted something done for him. He had come in by the back door, leaving his horse out back, and not opened his mouth until they were alone. From Overby's infrequent visits in the past, usually Whiteside had gleaned a moderate profit.

He answered, "Staked? I never staked anybody in my life. Those slopers had money to pay, hell knows how. I fixed 'em up to go over the hill, and they're long gone. Yeah, I've still got their monkey suits somewhere round."

"And a couple of men to wear 'em?" Overby's voice was soft.

"What kind?"

". . . Shooters."

Whiteside reached up and pushed the derby back on his head, glancing to front and rear before querying, "Who's elected?"

"The squaw man we brought in last night. He's camping up at the stage station."

"I know. Saw him pass by here today. He on the warpath?"

Overby eyed the man. The question was out of bounds and, deciding that Whiteside wasn't to be trusted with the slightest hint of a reason for the killing, he said, "There's a hundred dollars in it."

"Each," said Whiteside succinctly. "And a hundred for me. The monkey suits—"

Passing riders on the street caught his notice through the dingy front window, and he cut a look that way. "There he goes now," he mentioned. "With the DeBray girl."

Overby had already seen them and, although he could not make out their faces through the grime of the window, he imagined they were talking and smiling to each other. The mere sight of them together aroused a resurgence of the chill rage that had filled him when Victoria announced that she was riding with Sam Hatch.

"Three hundred it is!" he snapped.

Making private conjecture, Whiteside hid his quickened interest behind a bland inexpressiveness. "It's fifty for the monkey suits. Each."

"Four hundred, then, damn you! But it's got to be done right away."

"For cash, quick service," said Whiteside. "It's as good as done."

Sam returned in an unsettled state from riding back to Sunrise with Victoria. Not a word had passed between them all the way to the layout; he in a grim humor over Dwyer's loose talk, she in deep preoccupation. He supposed that coming upon Manuelito like that may have helped create an aversion in her. He was associated in her mind with the unwashed old reprobate. And, too, perhaps the laughter of Capi and Naka and their sudden hush contributed to it.

But when they had reached the layout and were turning in at the yard gate Victoria abruptly drew rein. Sam did the same, and their horses came to a stand under the crossbeam of the arch. She spoke then all in a rush, evidently unable to contain it a single instant longer.

"I have no business asking . . . I've no right to know! None whatever—" She held her face turned away from him, and what he could see of one cheek was in high color. “But—I want to know!”

“Yes?”

“What are those two Indian girls to you?”

It seemed to Sam a disproportionate amount of importance to attach to the question. “Capi is the sister of my dead wife, and Naka is my daughter,” was his economical reply. “They are the last of my band.”

Victoria then did a puzzling thing. She exclaimed “Oh!”—whether in embarrassment or anger, or both, Sam couldn’t tell—and then brought her braided quirt down on the flank of the black-and-white pinto, which shot forward. Sam started to follow and drew up. He watched her ride to the house, and then he wheeled and rode off before she had time to dismount and look back at him.

She was an impetuous young woman, he mused, letting the bay run. All manner of impulses beneath that cool poise. If all white women were anything like her, a man would never know where he stood.

So it was with no easy frame of mind that he rode up to the stage station, to find Manuelito reeling about the yard, jug in hand, chanting a fiery *samadia-sinan.* It didn’t require much to see that the old man was drunk. He apparently had finished the jug. And while Sam looked on, lips compressed, Dr. Dwyer came weaving forth from the harness shed as drunk as Manuelito, although he wasn't chanting.

"God's sake!" Sam roared.

Dwyer got himself righted, located Sam on his horse alongside the stage station, and hailed him cheerily. "Say, Hatch! Say! I discovered a jug earlier today—"

"Mine!"

"—cunningly buried in the wagon barn. I've a great gift for delving to the bottom of things, y'know. Great gift. Couldn't quite reach to the bottom of that jug, though. Gave the rest to the Indian, he looked so sad."

"Now look at him!"

The doctor squinted. "Look at him," he echoed. Manuelito was naked except for a loin cloth. "A living picture of mindless abandon, of abringal . . . ab-or-in-ig-al—" It was a measure of his condition that he had trouble in speaking correctly. "That is to say—"

Sam called, "Capi! Naka! You all right?"

Their faces appeared at an open window beside him. They looked prim and self-contained, clean as new pins, and very, very cool-eyed. "We are well." Capi spoke in Sioux, disdaining the English words she had learned from him. "You worry for us? Why?"

"Because—"

She closed the shutter of the window on his reply with a firm bang.

He stared at the shutter, amazed, his anger rising in him. God's sake! Capi was becoming as perverse as Victoria. A man didn't have to get among white women to put his mind in a muddle. Hell, they were all alike. Even little Naka . . .

Sam nudged the bay on past the building into the open yard. Noticing him for the first time and somehow mistaking him for an oncoming foe, Manuelito heaved the jug at him. The jug fell short, striking the bay's right foreleg a glancing blow and rolling under its feet, and the big horse reared back pawing.

Just then, from the margin of timber capping the nearest overlooking hill, two bursts of smoke bloomed from rifles in the hands of a pair of men whose dark blue garb sported brass buttons.

TEN

Sam jerked at the lashlike sting of a bullet tearing his chest. The other bullet whipped past his face and went screaming on.

He heard the whacking explosions of the rifles and, cutting a look toward the sound, he saw the pair of blue-clad men standing in sight at the edge of timber, lining their weapons to repeat fire. They were shooting to kill, up there.

Fierce knowledge of his danger tightened him. He was a clear target here in the open yard, and he quit the rearing bay under him fast, kicking both stirrups loose and sliding backward, making an ungainly landing on the ground. The momentum threw him off balance. Arms spread and boot heels digging, he pistoned his long legs and took a backward-running fall behind the shelter of the station as the rifles discharged their second shells.

Dr. Dwyer was standing dumfounded, rapidly sobering but his wits disordered. The bay came down on all fours and trotted a few paces, snorting, and Dwyer blinked at the animal as if it might tell him what was going on. Sam yelled at him, “Take cover, you damn fool!”

Regaining his wits, Dwyer walked hastily to the harness shed, where he hovered inside the doorway, looking out. No bullet sped his way, and Sam knew for certain then that the target was himself alone, nobody else.

The front of his flannel shirt stuck to him, blood-soaked. He had been breathing shallowly, and now he consciously took in air deeply, held it, and let it out. No pain inside his chest. The burning hurt was outside. Very well . . .

He had his six gun, but his rifle, a single-shot Sharps .50, hung on his saddle. Suicide to try for it. And it holding only the one load . . . Two men. He risked a quick look around the corner of the station. Still there, rifles now braced against trees, ready, waiting. At seventy yards he couldn't duel it out with his six gun. They wouldn't wait long. The sun was going down. Nothing to prevent them from splitting up, working around on two sides. Having tried so determinedly to drop him, first shots, and come so close to doing it, they weren't at all likely to give it up.

On the other hand the front of the station was blind to them. He could make a dash from there to rougher ground. Stalk them. He nodded to himself. Shorten the distance to pistol range before they picked him off. . . .

Manuelito, who had darted off at the first shots, now reappeared carrying his stolen Winchester repeater. Right in the yard, as conspicuous as a crow on a snowbank, he stood crouched, peering about for something to shoot.

“Give me that rifle!” Sam called to him urgently. “Quick!”

Manuelito was not giving up his rifle to anybody. He was unsteady and fuddled with whisky, and he plainly conceived this to be a personal fight of his, possibly a fight of fifty years ago. Muttering, he glared this way and that. His eyesight was not what it once must have been. He had trekked too many deserts. But in his ancient black eyes was the tigcr-flash that said he saw himself as an invincible buck in the fighting prime of life.

Laughter, harsh and jeering, floated down the hill. The two marksmen up there were seeing him as a skinny little scarecrow, a decrepit relic ludicrously gibbering futile threats.

Manuelito still had keen hearing. His ears aided his eyes to pick out the pair, and he gave a hair-raising howl as ferociously strong as Sam had ever heard. It was a howl of furious indignation. The Winchester repeater snapped up. Manuelito laid wizened cheek to walnut stock and took aim.

Dwyer called something to him from the door of the harness shed, unintelligible, made so by the crashing reports of the rifles on the hill, the two men up there revising their viewpoint in a hurry and firing simultaneously.

The Winchester stayed silent. It fell forward and away, Manuelito flinging it convulsively in his brief death throes. The scrawny old brave crumpled and lay twitching.

"Goddam!" came Dwyer's shaken voice. "I tried to tell him to drop it! They're soldiers! Hatch—"

"To hell with what they are!" Sam snarled, and ran out, firing his six gun up the hill.

He shot high, in hopes of dropping a bullet close enough to them to spoil their aim. Whether he succeeded, or whether it was his sudden erupting with a thudding gun that caused them to flinch, their shots came a shade late after him, whining past behind his flying figure. He snatched up the fallen Winchester and dodged on behind the harness shed to the rear corner, where he sank down on one knee and edged into position.

"Soldiers!" Dwyer was crying through the wall to him, all aghast. He appeared to feel that Sam was committing high treason. "You can't fire on soldiers, Hatch! It's—"

"The hell I can't!" Sam loosed a shot. "They fired on me, and they fired first!"

He clipped a cavalry hat and, after that, couldn't get in anything like a good crack at either of them. They had seen his retrieve of the Winchester, and were hugging cover, not allowing him another chance. They were in the shade of the trees, he in the slanting sunshine. He hadn't the advantage of being able to move about, as they had. He spent two more shells on speculation and scored nothing. Their return fire gouged splinters from the shed and whipped the dirt.

This wouldn't do. It was no good. No spare shells for the Winchester, and if Manuelito had had any he didn't know where they were and couldn't get at them even if he did know. That pair appeared to be well supplied.

Wrath did not overwhelm his judgment, and now he wondered at their firing at him without warning, why they were so intent upon killing him. A price on his head, he supposed, dead or alive, and they were out to earn it. He was not prepared to let them have it. He looked about him.

East of that yard the ground, thickly furred in undergrowth and studded with boulders, sloped downward to a crease that ran jaggedly northward. It would do, would have to do. He fired one more shot to duck the heads of the two and made his run, hitting the slope rolling, crashing through undergrowth, and fetching up against a half-buried boulder with a force that brought a grunt from him.

There, listening, he took out his six gun, reloaded, and holstered it. He had lost his hat but not the rifle. One shell was still left in it, and he levered it into the breech. He let himself on down the rest of the slope, and here he was out of sight of the pair, and he struck off up the crooked crease. Soon it deepened into a dry draw. He estimated that he was abreast of the timber-capped hill and, climbing the bank of the draw, he saw the trees come up closer than he had expected.

He climbed more cautiously then. The slant of the ground altered. He was going up the hill itself, having to dodge from boulder to boulder; the edge of timber ahead, down on his left the stage station and the body of old Manuelito starkly discernible in the yard.

"I'll get them for that," he murmured. They could have ducked to cover when the old man threw up his rifle. His killing had been brutally wanton.

Before him were no more boulders, and between him and the edge of timber lay a bare shoulder of hill. He ascended watchfully, his boots swishing softly in the dry grass. A movement stilled him, and he had a moment of gripping tension at the thought that he was standing here without an inch of cover. Something rose stealthily, bulging from a tree trunk, then froze rigid an instant before a nerve-strained voice yelled thinly:

"Look out! There he—!"

The bulge became the shape of a man all in a flurry, bringing up elbows and rifle, and with the muzzle-flare spurting out at him, Sam fired. The man bent, stumbled a pace, straightened up again. Sam dropped the emptied Winchester and stroked out his six gun. He was conscious of the booming report of another rifle at a distance, like a single delayed echo, but took no time looking to find its source.

The man ahead of him twisted half around, as if hit by a rock, legs tangling, hands flung out. He fell and rolled over twice downhill and lay with his arms sprawled. Silence came, shortly broken by the lifting hoofbeats of two horses racing through the timber. Sam triggered four quick-spaced shots from his six gun into the trees. The pounding of the hoofs continued, suddenly fading off. The horses had put the hill behind them.

Sam looked down to his left then to see Dr. Dwyer trudging up toward where he stood. And beyond Dwyer, at the stage station, Capi and Naka.

Capi was on her knees, leaning against the back wall of the station. The single-shot Sharps .50 lay on the ground before her, a faint wisp of powder smoke still trickling from its muzzle. She was rubbing her right shoulder. Naka was leaning over her, clearly concerned only for Capi's hurt. That heavy Sharps had a brutal kick.

Dwyer, puffing short-breathed and shaking his head, came up to Sam, groaning dismally, "You and Capi have killed a soldier! And the other got away to tell of it, eh? Bad, bad . . . !"

Sam eyed him steadily. "Capi?" he said. "She

didn't shoot, didn't touch a gun. It was me. Understand?"

The doctor nodded after meeting Sam's eyes. He was sober now, sickly sober. "All right, if you—"

"She didn't touch a gun," Sam repeated, a hard edge to his voice, his face flinty. "Remember that! If you ever—!"

Dwyer said quietly. "There are limits even to my indiscretions. Your Capi had nothing whatever to do with this, Hatch, and I'll swear to it on the Bible if I'm asked."

Sighing, he followed Sam to the blue-clad body. The dead man had a mean face, a ferret face, with a narrow black mustache and two parallel scars reaching from left ear to jaw line. And Dwyer, taking closer look, exclaimed, "God-dam!"

"Now what?" Sam asked him.

"I know this sorry bird! Hell, he's no soldier! His name's One-Thumb Nalley, and he hangs around Despré."

"You sure?"

"Sure as I'm alive. See, his left thumb's missing. That's why I noticed him. Seen him in Whiteside's poison shop. It's him, all right. Hah!" Having ascertained that the dead man wasn't a soldier, Dwyer was disposed to dismiss the matter: "Well, that's different. Drag him off and cave a gully bank over him and forget him."

Sam felt in no way satisfied to let it go at that. In a hoodlum hangout such as Despré a couple of thugs, gunmen, might very well set out to murder and rob any stranger they considered worth it. But that didn't explain the army uniforms. Nor why they had not fired at Dwyer when they had every opportunity to do so. No, robbery couldn't have been their motive. They had simply sought to kill him, and it seemed as if they had wanted Dwyer alive as witness that soldiers did the killing. Why?

It opened up a speculative train of thought. Sam put it aside, however, and, picking up the Winchester, he walked with Dwyer back down to the stage station. The puzzle could be solved later.

In the yard, examining Sam's wound by the failing light, Dwyer grunted, "Bullet sliced a nice groove across your chest. A couple inches back and you'd be dead."

Sam agreed. Manuelito, tossing that jug at him and causing the bay to rear back, had unknowingly saved his life.

Curiously enough, the doctor, like Naka, paid his chief concern to Capi. Ever so gently he turned back her buckskin jacket and shirt and touched the softly rounded shoulder with compassionate fingers—fingers that, examining Sam's wound, had been briskly businesslike. Capi did not flinch, but Dwyer was looking into her dark eyes, and they apparently told him what he needed to know.

"Come into my place, and I'll put some liniment on it," he said to her. "Ease the stiffness. It'll be black and blue tomorrow. You come in too, Hatch, and I'll slap a bandage on you."

Sam, standing with head bent over dead Manuelito, nodded. "Laughed at him and shot him down," he said bitterly. Manuelito, cross-grained, often sullen, had fallen out with him many times, and hadn't ever been worth his keep. But the old Apache outcast had called him brother and been ready when sober to fight by his side to the death. "If only they hadn't laughed at him—"

In the Lucky Jack the following noon, Whiteside said to Tobe Overby, "A surprise to me. And," he added dryly, "a surprise to Nalley and Preston too! Rattled? Preston looked sick when he got back here."

Overby smacked fist in palm, demanding, "But how could they mess up a single job like that? All they had to do was wait there and shoot!"

"Well"—Whiteside shrugged—"it didn't go off that way. From what I get out of Preston, your squaw man was stalking them before they knew it. They knocked over the old Indian, and that was all they scored, though Preston thinks they winged your man."

"Does he say if Hatch knew they weren't soldiers?"

The saloonman shook his head. "Preston's gone. Can't say I blame him. Wouldn't want that big cuss on *my* trail."

Glowering at him, Overby drew his thoughts together. If Hatch did know that the pair had not been soldiers he'd be casting about for the answer to why they tried to kill him. And if DeBray heard of it after his threat to blow the works— But it was a thousand to one that Hatch had never seen Nalley before. Then a cold apprehension touched Overby, and sharply he put another question to Whiteside.

"Did the doc know Nalley?"

The saloonman fingered the greasy brim of his derby and cogitated. "He's been in here when Nalley was here. Doubt he took any note of him. No reason why he would."

Overby cursed under his breath. "We've got to find out for sure. Pump him next time he comes in. Get him drunk, and he'll talk."

"He always buys a bottle and off he—"

"Get him drunk, I said, damn it! Pump him!"

The Sunrise ramrod's ugly tone and stare quelled Whiteside and, bobbing his head in prompt assent, he said, "I don't take to tell any man his business, least of all you— But look. We're due for another raid from Fort Reno, rounding up boomers. If—"

"We've got our scouts out," Overby interrupted.

"Sure, I know. But if this Hatch don't get the warning like the rest—then what? He's wanted. He'll be took. Maybe not alive—he's quick on the fight, the way he went after Nalley and Preston."

The last thing Overby wanted was for Sam Hatch to be taken alive to Fort Reno. Hatch's answers to questions put to him there could easily start Colonel Buskirk along a line of deduction harking back to the old mystery of the Skeleton Creek massacre.

Overby stared so steadily and unblinkingly at Whiteside that the saloonman edged uneasily from the back edge of the bar with keen recollections of this gaunt man's numerous outbursts of vicious violence. But what Tobe Overby was thinking was: Hatch won't be taken alive if he thinks he's killed a soldier. If, on the other hand, he knows Nalley was bogus, he'll likely jump to the conclusion that the next soldiers coming at him also are bogus, and he'll open fire.

"And if he slips clear," Overby murmured aloud, "we can fix a way to let Krahn have him." And he frowned. Why hadn't he thought of the Circle K owner before? Krahn and his tough crew would rejoice to get Hatch into their hands.

"H'm?" Whiteside peered at him questioningly through his puffy lids.

“Don’t forget about the doc,” Overby ordered him curtly, and paced out.

The moment he left the Lucky Jack, his thoughts turned to Victoria. He was riding his splendid black horse today, and the animal feared him, and that was what brought Victoria to his mind. He had been told on all sides that he couldn’t break the black when he bought it. But he had broken it. He kept it toeing the mark with a curved spade bit and a metal burr, and crisp mornings when the horse started out snuffy he used the refined cruelty of a ghost cord on it.

He wrenched the reins back tight now, mounting, and used the spur mercilessly and was riding at a lope within ten yards of start, his customary fashion. Women, he ruminated unemotionally, were more easily broken than horses. He would force matters with Victoria.

Once having penetrated Capi’s reserve by treating her bruised shoulder, Dr. Dwyer frankly exhibited an unexpected fondness for hers and Naka’s company and, what was more remarkable, they for his.

Sam came upon the doctor down on his knees, a pointed stick in his hand, scratching in the dirt of the yard. Capi and Naka, also on their knees and likewise armed with pointed sticks, were copying exactly the doctor’s movements. Sam had been doing a burying job, and he inquired a bit tartly, “What’s going on here?”

Dwyer glanced up at him briefly. “I was teaching Naka the alphabet,” he replied, “and Capi became interested and joined the class.”

He drew the letter Q in the dust. Capi and Naka, perhaps self-conscious or else too absorbed to look up at Sam, faithfully copied it. “That’s called *kū*,” the doctor told them, and they both repeated softly, “Kū . . .”

As Sam still stood there Dwyer said to him somewhat gruffly, “Don’t you want them to learn white ways like you? Or are you leaving them behind?”

Stung, Sam retorted, “I brought them along with me from—”

“I mean in a different sense,” said Dwyer. “They’re both intelligent. They’re quick learners.” He scratched the R, S, and T. “Watch them. It’s a long way from learning the first A B C’s to reading the classics, but millions have done it. Even you, dumb as you are!” And to the girls as they finished scratching accurate letters with their sticks: “That’s *är*, and that’s *ĕs*, and that’s *tē* . . .” They echoed the sounds after him.

Sam gazed down on the bent heads of the two girls. He felt awkward and blunderingly intrusive, but he looked on while Dwyer progressed to Z. For the first time he had a feeling that he was not of supreme importance to Capi and Naka, that he was being left out. He should have experienced relief at the loosening of responsibility, the lessening of their utter dependence upon him, and instead it gave him a queer sense of loss.

Dwyer got to his feet, grunting, brushing his trousers. "So much for the block letters, the capitals. Get them straight and next I'll show you how to make the small letters. Hatch, they learn fast. They don't forget."

"Indians have good memories," Sam said abstractedly.

"Goddam it, forget they're Indians! They're people!" It was a surprising rebuke, coming from Dwyer, who in the first place had strongly urged Sam to put his Indian family out of his mind.

"You're the one who—" Sam began dryly.

"I know, I know," Dwyer broke in hastily. "By the way, I've been thinking about Nalley and whoever was his helper. They weren't smart, or they'd have blacked their faces. I happen to know there's only a skeleton company of white soldiers left in Fort Reno, and they're in administration. Negro troops, like those you escaped from, do all the patrolling. White officers."

"I hated having to pull that on the corporal," Sam mentioned. "The colonel struck me as a man who'd be hard on him."

"Colonel Buskirk," said Dwyer, "is new to the post. His job is to clean out this part of the Territory. Too many boomers and riffraff floating in. Too much trouble between cattlemen, and too few of them holding legitimate grazing permits. I heard the colonel, when I was at Fort Reno, state his intention to take to the field personally and see to it that the job gets done. The former commander was easygoing. Buskirk is a cracking hard man, one of the Department's toughest trouble shooters."

Sam nodded. He could well believe it, and an icy claw plucked his stomach at the reminder that he himself was being especially sought for by that remorseless officer with all his widespread resources.

"Going back to Nalley and the other one," he said to Dwyer, "I've been thinking, too. They had no reason for trying that on me. Somebody must've put them up to it, somebody who wants me dead. Who? Overby? He's the only man I've had anything like a run-in with here. But what would be his motive? Anyway, much as the sight of him raises my hackles, I will say he doesn't strike me as the kind of man who'd hire his killings done for him."

"He's not," Dwyer agreed. As for the question of motive, he was thinking his own thoughts. A woman such as Victoria DeBray could provide sufficient motive.

"Tell you what," Dwyer proposed after a minute. "Nalley hung out in the Lucky Jack a lot. I'll amble in there tonight when there's a crowd and listen to the talk. Might pick up something."

Might pick up a bender, Sam thought uncharitably, and do all the talking. "Maybe we should let it drop," he countered. "I'll be moving on before long. Can't stay here. Let it go."

"No, no!" Dwyer shook his head. "I may stumble on something tonight—"

"Stumble is the right word."

"It's worth my trying," Dwyer said, not hearing Sam's interpolation. He had a faraway look in his eyes, and he dragged the tip of his tongue over his lower lip.

That was around midday. The afternoon Dwyer spent actually instructing Capi how to design dresses for herself and Naka from the dress goods that Sam had purchased for them with such vain results during the long trek out of Texas. Dwyer sketched the designs from his memories, he said, of officers' wives on army posts, dance-hall belles, and, farther back, women in Eastern cities. It appeared that he possessed an observant and critical eye in that respect.

After lengthy study of his own sketches he measured Capi and Naka, using a knotted string of yarn, and confidently explained how the dress goods should be cut with scissors from his medical kit. He stood over Capi while she worked, encouraging and cautioning her gravely, as though overseeing a surgical operation.

That Capi and Naka were having the time

of their lives was very clear. They dropped every vestige of reserve, and their laughter and excited exclamations filled the stage station. Their shining eyes regarded the down-at-heel, life-battered little doctor as one gifted beyond common mortals, a great man, a genius . . .

Sam wasn't sure but what they were right. He stepped around gingerly like any overawed male in a dressmaker's parlor, struck speechless and feeling more than ever out of it.

ELEVEN

Sam was anything but a heavy sleeper at any time, and he slept so lightly that night he stayed half-conscious of the workings of his mind. Dr. Dwyer had gone off on foot the quarter mile to Despré and the Lucky Jack hours ago. No foretelling the results of that. Drinking and loquacious . . . spilling streams of garbled fact and fancy . . .

He came up wide awake, listening. Something had moved outside in the yard, making a slight rustle of sound. There was hardly any breeze. Capi and Naka slept in the next room, no door between. He listened intently for their regular even breathing, and his ears caught the sound outside again. If it was Dwyer getting back from Despré he was being unusually quiet about it. A stumbling man couldn't move that quietly, and to expect Dwyer to return sober was beyond all reason.

The moon shone aslant through the unshuttered window into the room. Sam reached to his gun belt on the floor and slid the gun from its holster. He had removed only boots and belt before lying down and, avoiding the window, he padded noiselessly to the rear doorway—it had no door; he peered out, gun in hand.

A figure cloaked loosely in some pale material stood motionless in the bare yard. It gave him a shock. Then, moonlight behind the still figure showing him the head crowned with a golden halo of hair, Sam got his second shock.

"Victoria!" He stepped swiftly forward.

"Sam . . . !" She half tottered to meet him, and he caught her, thinking that she was about to fall. "Oh, Sam—Sam, I'm so frightened!" She was shaking uncontrollably in his arms, speaking to him in sobbing whispers. "I ran—all the whole way here . . . And there was no light. And I didn't know what to—"

She broke down, sobbing against him, on the edge of collapse, her voice choking off in her throat. Sam picked her up off her feet and carried her to the harness shed, into Dwyer's quarters. It seemed somehow the best place. He sat her on Dwyer's homemade bunk. He found the lantern, matches, lighted it and hung it up, and shutting the door he looked at Victoria.

She wore a green silk dressing robe over a nightgown of lighter green, and the lower folds of both flimsy garments hung torn and dusty. Sam had thought that her feet were bare, as were his own, but she had on green slippers of quilted silk. The little slippers, never meant for touching rough ground, were ruined. She was exhausted physically and emotionally, but overwrought nerves would not let her relax, and she sat shaking, hands tightly clasped and the beauty of her face marred by intense strain.

Sam untwined Victoria's fingers and took her hands firmly in his. Seating himself beside her on the bunk, he said, "Breathe in deeply . . . Hold it . . . Now let it out, slowly—slowly . . . Again . . ."

She obeyed, turning her head and meeting his steady gaze. Presently the shaking began to subside, and her hands were less rigid. Sam rose and brought her a dipper of cold water from Dwyer's pail beside the stove. The stove, made from an iron drum, its flue a series of connected tin cans, still retained a few red embers, and he added some chunks of kindling. He was giving Victoria time to pull herself together.

Reseating himself beside her, he asked then, "Call you tell me now what's happened?"

She said, "Yes," in an uncertain tone. And following a pause: "Tobe Overby—!"

Sam's face hardened. Overby again. "What—?"

"I was in bed. Something woke me. It wasn't a noise. It was something else—a horrible feeling of—" Her breath caught, and she swallowed. "He was climbing in my bedroom window, quiet as a cat! And I saw his face—!" Her hands flew up to cover her eyes.

"Go on," Sam said tonelessly.

"I was terrified. Waking up suddenly like that—He was so quiet. And his face . . . his expression!

I couldn't even scream, I was so frightened. And my father—he had taken some of that sleeping medicine. I'd looked in on him earlier, and he was lying as though unconscious. Overby must have known that somehow. And Maria was spending the night with her sister's sick children."

"Are there any guns in the house?"

"I never thought of them. I didn't even think of the men sleeping in the bunkhouses. I snatched up my robe and slippers. He was inside the window by then— Not a sound! Not a word! Glaring at me—and smiling! I rushed out of the house. He was after me. I could *feel* him coming after me! I didn't dare to look back. All I could think of was to get here. So—so I came here, running all the way—"

"Through Despré?"

"I went around. It was the brush and the broken ground that—" Her tears gushed, and Sam put his arms around her, and she clung to him.

She was not equipped to cope with an experience like that, he was thinking. Running terrified in the night. A mile and a quarter in those pitifully inadequate bedroom slippers. Pursued by a man with the atrociously brutal instincts of a marijuana-mad Yaqui buck.

"Did Overby follow you here?" Sam asked her. He hoped so.

"No." She shook her head on his chest, mumbling between spasms of crying. "I had the feeling after a while that he'd lost me and didn't know where I had gone."

She managed shortly to stem the weeping, but the shuddering returned, worse than before. "Sam!" she gasped. "Give me something! I'm shaking to pieces! I'm—cold!" Yet the shed was becoming overwarm as the fresh fuel roared in the stove. "Give me something, Sam!"

There was no whisky in the shed. Sam ran a helpless glance over Dr. Dwyer's array of pharmaceutical jars and containers, totally unacquainted with their contents and labels. "Wait here, I'll only be gone a minute," he told Victoria, and went across to the stage station.

He tugged on his boots while there. In the adjoining room someone stirred—Capi or Naka—and he waited briefly before picking up the old painted parfleche and leaving. Recrossing the yard, he followed an obscure impulse to look back at the station and thought that the moonlit window of his room framed a pale round blur just above the level of the high sill, but looking harder he saw nothing and guessed he must have imagined it.

In the wagon shed he heated a half inch of water in a pan on the stove. He opened up the parfleche and pored reflectively over the dozens of little buckskin pouches. Some wolfsbane, yes, and hop seed . . . buchu too, and a pinch of aromatic wild bergamot. He measured by eye the dried herbs and dropped them into the hot water, and when the steeping was finished he poured off the liquid into a cup and handed it to Victoria.

Her hands were shaking too badly, so he held it to her lips while she sipped. She got it all down, making a face over the last of it. Sam emptied the pan and rinsed out it and the cup. He restrapped the parfleche and slid it out of the way. The potion that he had given Victoria should now begin having some effect. He looked at her.

Victoria sat relaxed, not shivering in the slightest, her bare ankles crossed and her hands in her lap. Her face had color. There even were tiny beads of perspiration forming on her forehead. That was the buchu. She was smiling faintly, and, lips parted, she met Sam's look, her ice-green eyes lustrous. And that was the combination of wolfsbane, hop seed— Her system evidently had a very low tolerance for narcotics, even the mildest, and Sam thought: "Thank the stars I didn't give her anything powerful!"

What she needed now was fresh air before the heat inside the shed overcame her, and Sam said, "I'll saddle my horse and another for you and see you home."

She fingered her robe and nightgown. Her color heightened. "I can't very well ride a straight saddle like this, Sam."

"Well, then," he said, seeing the point, "I'll fold

a blanket, and you can sit sideways up behind me."

She considered it dreamily. "I hate going back there."

He thought, And I hate taking you back, but . . . Aloud, he said, "It—uh—I think it's best." Then more briskly, "Lock your bedroom door and shutter the window. And keep a loaded gun on hand. Every night. *Every* night, Victoria, from now on."

"Yes, Sam." She stood up, exhaling a sigh that ended on a kind of small moan. "Whatever you say."

"I'll go saddle up now."

"Whatever you say. And, Sam . . ."

He was at the door. ". . . Yes?"

"Call me Vicky."

"I'll be happy to—Vicky."

He was gone then, and she buried her burning face in her hands. "Shameless!" she whispered. "Shameless hussy! What has come over me? I've never, *never*— Am I losing my mind?"

Beyond the arched gateway all the buildings of the Sunrise layout stood as dark-shadowed angles in the moonlight, black on milky gray, and the hoofs of the walking bay horse threw beats of magnified sound into the wide silence.

As before, the mile-and-quarter trip had been accomplished without conversation, though this time with the difference that for Victoria it was impossible to cloak herself in aloofness while forced to hold onto Sam in order to keep her seat behind him. The effects of Sam's potion had not yet worn off her, either, and were causing her to yawn drowsily. But she had her nerves in hand. Nothing more was going to frighten her out of her senses, not this night at least.

Sam reined up to the shadowed front of the house and reached back a helping arm for Victoria to alight. He swung down out of saddle to stand with her, and the parting moment found them both voiceless. Neither one could find anything suitable to say, yet they stood rooted, each waiting for the other to make an appropriate break that would allow Victoria to go on into the house and Sam to take his leave.

An unseen spark flashing between them dissolved the deadlock, Sam making his compulsive step, taking Victoria into his arms, and kissing her on the mouth. For the fraction of a second Victoria stood as marble, then her lips were readily responsive.

"Sam!" she breathed.

Hardly had she begun the low murmur before he felt her suddenly stiffen. She was staring wide-eyed over his shoulder and, releasing her, Sam spun around, seeing first a man's long moon shadow on the ground, next the man: Tobe Overby.

Overby had come silently around the side of

the house, and he stood in moonlight. He held a gun in his fist, held it trained dead-center at Sam's heart. Rage deepened and twisted the lines of his gaunt face. The leaden sheen of his eyes was inhuman. He spoke to Victoria in a hoarse, snarling whisper:

"Stand clear, woman!"

Under the virulent force of his command Victoria moved two paces off from Sam and stopped. Sam had left his holster belt back at the stage station. His gun was thrust into his waistband on his left side, and to reach it demanded a cross draw. He inwardly cursed his singular lapse of wariness, the folly of allowing himself to be caught unprepared and incautious here on Sunrise. All Overby had to do was squeeze trigger.

"Tobe!"—it was Victoria speaking—"if you kill Sam—I'll tell what happened tonight!" And that betrayed the fact that she would not otherwise tell of it, for fear of the explosion between her sick father and Overby, and its consequences. Her father was no match whatever for his foreman in a collision.

"And what happened tonight?" Overby's voice was a deadly monotone.

"I'll tell you." Sam spoke, stalling for time, watching that steady gun. "You crawled in her window, and she had to run. She ran to me—"

"You're lying, or she dreamed it." Contempt

edged the monotone. "It's a poor way of trying to cover up a—"

"What?" It was an indignant exclamation from Victoria, but the Sunrise ramrod chose to take it as a query.

His leaden eyes traveled up and down her robe and nightgown. "Shall I put it in plain words? Your night out! With a squaw man! A sorry disgrace to Sunrise! I got no license to deal with you as you should be dealt with. But I can sure fix *his* wagon! I'll never get a better chance than this!"

Those last words of Overby's clicked in Sam's mind: *I'll never get a better chance* . . . Overby, then, sought that chance and now found it placed unexpectedly in his hands. He was going to use it. Nobody on Sunrise would blame him. It would be hushed up. As for Victoria's accusation against him—for a charge, a countercharge. Few if any would believe her, probably not even her father. An erring woman lying preposterously in frantic effort to save her reputation. He, Sam Hatch, had brought her home in her night clothes, and they had been caught together in— No, Overby would never get a better chance. The loyal avenger of Sunrise honor!

On that thought Sam tensed his right arm for the cross draw.

"If you kill Sam—!" Victoria repeated desperately.

On the point of shooting, Overby slid his eyes back to her and inquired sardonically, "You'll tell your fancy tale? Who'll believe it? You ran to him, he said. All the way to the old stage station? You? No, no! Not the soft and sheltered Victoria DcBray!" He snuffled a humorless laugh. "You slipped out and met him, and the pair of you—"

"Look at her slippers," Sam cut in suddenly. "Worn down to shreds by the stones and gravel between here and the station! Look at the bottom of that nightgown—all torn by running through the brush around Despré! Step over in the moonlight, Vicky, and let him see."

She did so. Tobe Overby looked, and his face underwent a change. The condition of the slippers and gown offered conclusive evidence that Victoria had traversed that mile and a quarter on foot, part of it through the brush, running. And she, of all people, could scarcely be imagined as doing that to keep a tryst. Nor any woman in her right mind.

It shook Overby, made him unsure whether this, after all, was his perfect chance to get rid of Sam Hatch and present a plausible reason for his act. The longer he debated with himself over it, the less sure he became, and the more malignantly furious because of it.

"All right!" he muttered in a strangled voice. "All right!" But he couldn't let Sam Hatch go unscathed. Slam him down and stomp him. Not kill him. Cripple him. Just about as good. Hatch was trespassing by night on the Sunrise layout. Reason enough, and a crippled wreck with a crushed larynx couldn't bring about much harm thereafter.

Lowering his gun an inch or two, Overby moved a step forward, looking at Victoria's ruined slippers in imitation of a man not quite convinced by what he saw. Watching him, reading his eyes, Sam foresaw in a flash the forthcoming move. The slash of gun barrel across his jaw. The sledging downstroke on his temple. The rest to follow, boot heels expertly crunching him. Overby, the doctor had said, was a devil who enjoyed kicking his victims to broken hulks.

The jawbreaking upsweep of the gun barrel did not catch Sam off his guard, but it was a blur of motion so fast that he hooked his left arm up barely in time to block it. His elbow and under-muscles took the blow, and fierce pain knifed through that arm from fingers to shoulder. It knocked him backward a stride. From Victoria came a small and helpless cry of dismay.

Overby followed through instantly, whipping a long stroke at him in a tigerish frenzy to smash Sam down and get to work on him. Sam's left arm was painful and awkward, slow to his will. He snapped his right arm up and over. His outspread fingers met the wrist of Overby's descending arm and closed tight, and he flung himself in an about-face, twisting it. Overby grunted in agony and collided into Sam's back, and they both fell, Sam face down underneath.

The heavy fall broke Sam's grip on Overby's wrist. Sam heaved Overby off his back and, rolling over, he came up in a crouch and lunged. His left arm slowed him. The Sunrise ramrod was quicker getting up and drove a kick at Sam's face while Sam was yet hunched. Sam dodged, the sharp high boot heel skinning his cheek, and reached for his gun.

His waistband held no gun. The weapon had dropped out in the fall somewhere; and no time to look down for it. He saw then that Overby, kicking madly at him, had empty hands, that the twisted wrist had forced Overby's fingers open, letting his gun go. Sam leaped at him. His driving weight smashed into him, and as he staggered back from the impact, Sam's right fist tilted his head hard askew with a crack alongside the jaw.

He thought he had him set up then for a quick finish, but the man was iron. Before Sam could get his right fist cocked to hit him again, the ramrod had regained balance and was coming at him, and now he was coolly weaving, using shifty footwork, ring-fashion, a style of fighting unfamiliar to Sam.

Sam lifted both arms, his left sluggish, to meet the attack. It was his left, though, that stopped the force of a reaching, pistonlike punch. Fresh pain shot through his arm, and he had to let it down, and for that moment he felt a fear that Overby could get him. Instead of pressing in, however, the man circled him, jabbing and chopping to wear him down and edging him away from where their guns had fallen.

Sam stepped into the punishing punches, swinging, his right fist smearing Overby's mouth red and the next blow thudding in below the chest. Overby doubled low and half turned away, giving out a groan, suddenly snatching down at the ground, and bringing up a gun. Sam kicked at it.

The pointed and hard-packed toe of his riding boot struck gun butt and fingers, and the gun sailed off, Overby coming upright, wincing shock on his bloodied face. Insensible now to pain, Sam tottered him with a left to the body and brought up his right, putting his weight behind it, flush on the jaw.

The Sunrise ramrod back-stepped clumsily, swaying, his leaden eyes glazed. From some reserve of vitality he steadied himself, planted his feet apart, and attempted a fighting stance. Sam grabbed him, spun him around, picked him up bodily, and hurled him to the ground. Breath burst from Overby's mouth with a whistling moan.

Sam stooped and picked him up again. He stood him on his feet and slammed him full in the face with his open right hand, sending him sprawling back to earth. Then he was done with it, and he looked toward Victoria to find her staring wide-eyed at him.

Thinking that she was aghast at him for savagery, he said harshly, "It's not a patch on what he'd have done to me if he'd got me down."

He became aware of noise coming from the two Sunrise bunkhouses behind the house and of dim reflections of lights springing up. The slugging had been heard. The men of the crew were tumbling out to investigate.

He walked to the bay horse and climbed stiffly into the saddle, his battered body aching. Looking again at Victoria, he told her, "Better go on in to your room. Don't forget the door and window. I doubt he'll feel up to any more window-prowling tonight, but lock them anyway."

She said nothing, simply staring at him, and with a murmured, "Good night, Vicky," he reined the bay horse around and took off, hitting a lope before reaching the arched gateway. When he looked back from there, men were gathering about Overby on the ground, and Victoria was nowhere to be seen.

TWELVE

Passing through Despré on the way to the stage station, Sam picked out the Lucky Jack along the single street, its faded sign still legible in the waning moonlight. He ran a neutral glancc over the shabby dive, noting that it was darkened and closed up, wondering what sort of evening Dr. Dwyer had spent in there.

Reaching the station, he stripped and tended to the bay, turned it into the horse pen, and walked to the harness shed. There was no light when he pushed open the door and entered. He struck a match and lighted the lantern and found that the doctor was lying fully dressed on his bunk.

Dwyer came awake with the light. He was drunk, but he had been a lot drunker in his life, and after a pull from a bottle which he groped out from under the bunk, he sat up rubbing his eyes and took cognizance of Sam.

"What happened to your face?" were his first words. "Looks like you stopped a train with it."

Sam cracked a sore grin. "You oughta see the other fella."

"Who?"

"Oh . . . Tobe Overby."

"Goddam!" ejaculated Dwyer. "That should've

been something to see." Taking another drink, he nursed the bottle between faintly trembling hands on his knees. "Where?"

"On Sunrise," Sam said sparely. "But never mind that now. You learn anything tonight in that broken-down deadfall?"

Dwyer eyed Sam's face a while longer, speculatively, but didn't push his curiosity, having learned that the big man would say just so much on a subject and no more.

Answering Sam's question, he said, "Frankly, not much. But Whiteside acted damn queer. He was pushing free drinks to me—which isn't a bit like Whiteside—and trying to lead me into talking. I made out to be drunker than I was and let drop a hint or two. His ears practically stretched every time I opened my mouth. Have a drink, Hatch?"

Sam swallowed some and flinched. "Tastes like liniment. I ought to rub some on me. My ribs don't feel good."

"I'll do that for you," Dwyer offered seriously. He went on, "Yes—friend Whiteside knows about your shoot-out with Nalley and his pal, and he wants to know more. I think the pal, by the way, was named Preston, an Arkansas dodger. He's skipped, owing money all round, on a horse not his own. There was talk about him in the crowd. It's likely that Whiteside acted as go-between. Hired that pair for somebody else."

Sam nodded. "For Overby, I'd say. Tomorrow I'll find out for sure."

"At the Lucky Jack?"

"Where else?"

Dwyer scanned Sam's cut and battered face, the skinned knuckles of his hands, and observed dryly, "For a quiet cuss who's positively not on the warpath, you certainly head into some fine hot jack pots, don't you?" And when Sam made no reply he said, "Oh, another thing I heard in the crowd. Soldiers from Fort Reno are reported working toward here, combing out boomers. The usual raid is looked for here in three or four days."

"Do they run to a pattern then?" Sam asked. "Doesn't sound smart of the soldiers."

The doctor smiled at his bottle. "It doesn't. But the fact is, Hatch, the soldiers know they're spotted long in advance, and they just don't try surprising Sunrise any more. Everybody who has no business being here scatters to the brush like quail. The soldiers make their search, pay a call on DeBray to give him official warning not to harbor boomers, and ride away empty-handed. It's a system rather than a pattern. The system is based on spies who depend, like the rest, on Sunrise for protection and a living. Overby's idea, I think. That man's no fool, and he's a natural-born leader and organizer."

"He's also a killer."

“That he is,” agreed Dwyer. “About the soldiers, though . . . We’ll get warning in time for you and the girls to duck out. But meantime you’d better hide the Indian belongings. Make sure there’s not a scrap left for the soldiers to find around here. And get rid of poor old Manuelito’s horse.”

“I’ll tend to it first thing in the morning,” Sam told him. “I’ll run the roan off and stow the stuff in the wagon up the arroyo.”

“Here it’s called a dry creek.”

“And gunmen are called boomers, home-steaders—”

“They’re not all gunmen, Hatch. Some are genuinely seeking to settle and farm. Too few, I’ll admit, but some.”

Whiteside was acutely uncomfortable. His bloated face was a bad color, and behind their puffy lids his sour, slitted eyes showed worry. His discomfort had risen on the instant that the big, dark man with fight-scarred face paced quietly into the Lucky Jack. Three gun-slung men, Despré dwellers, were loitering together at the bar, cutting cards for drinks, and Whiteside kept fingering the brim of his derby in a mute signal for them to stand by.

Not ordering a drink right away, Sam stood midway across the floor, looking the sorry place over. He took everything in before flicking his glance over the three customers and bringing it to rest on Whiteside. He moved on to the unclean bar then and nodded.

The saloonman reached beneath the bar, hesitated, and brought up a bottle and shot glass. He tilted bottle to glass, and while he was pouring, Sam spoke.

"One-Thumb Nalley was a friend of yours. And Preston."

Whiteside spilled whisky freely on the bar, shocked by the directness of Sam's statement. He set the bottle down, and shaking his head he said, "No. I got no friends, mister. Only customers. That'll be four bits."

"I believe you." Sam clinked a half dollar on the bar. "They were customers then—like these." He inclined his head sideways toward the three at the far end of the bar.

The three men were already conscious of something amiss from Whiteside's manner, and at Sam's reference to them they came alert. They ceased all conversation to listen, gazing down thoughtfully at their glasses, and the one having the deck of cards stilled his hands.

"Yeah, they were customers, Nalley and Preston," Whiteside responded, growing more confident. "Why?"

"You put a job their way. They fell down on it." Sam spoke quite casually. "Nalley's dead and Preston's gone. Who was it wanted that job done?"

Whiteside's face grayed. "What the hell are you talking about? I don't know anything about any job!" His eyes shuttled to the listening three. "Look, you—if you've come in here looking for trouble . . . !"

One of the three men called to him, "Fill 'em up again here, Whitey."

The saloonman, after a moment of indecision, made to reach below the bar. Sam said to him, "The bottle's right here."

The three swung slowly to face Sam, and the one who had spoken said, "We don't drink from that bottle."

"Then you don't drink," Sam said.

"You telling us?"

"I'm telling you."

The man shifted, stood out as spearhead of the trio, his look brightening with challenge, splayed hands denoting a thought for his gun. Seeing him shift, his two companions likewise got set.

Sam's blued-steel stare pinned them. Deadly warning lurked in his easy stance, in the manner in which he let his right arm hang down, left elbow on the bar, thumb and forefinger lightly holding the brimming shot glass level. And when Sam said in the same moderate tone that he had used before, "Better stay out of this," they grudgingly turned with one accord and faced the bar.

Whiteside had remained in his partly stooped position, frozen in his reach for his hidden weapon, eyes turned upward, and now Sam bent attention on him. He flipped the contents of the shot glass into the saloonman's pouchy face and in unbroken extension of the movement batted his derby off and grasped a large handful of his hair.

Whiteside yelped in pain, reaching both hands up to his stretched scalp. Sam yanked him mercilessly forward and forced his face down against the counter of the bar.

"Who was it wanted that job done on me?"

The saloonman squirmed and cursed. The three at the far end did not bring their heads around to look, only their eyes, for Sam's right arm still hung free, his hand an inch from gun butt.

"Who were you acting for, Whiteside?"

Whiteside stopped his squirming, as though to listen. The three men were raising their heads, too, in a listening attitude. Noises were breaking out in Despré. There were running footsteps, a confused shouting. Sam paid no heed to it.

"Talk," he said, "or I'll print your face right into the wood! Was it Overby? Talk—"

Then suddenly soldiers were filing into the Lucky Jack from front and rear, bearing carbines at the ready, and a leathery lieutenant of cavalry was barking, "Up with your hands, you men!"

Giving orders for the regular patrols to draw diversion by following their customary routine,

Colonel Buskirk had personally marched a detachment of troopers a hundred miles around the compass and swooped upon Sunrise from the southwest. Dr. Dwyer considered the maneuver most unfair and, being scarcely sober, he so proclaimed it, out loud and several times.

The doctor stood bareheaded in the yard of the stage station, confronting the colonel and a squad of the detachment. Capi and Naka stood silently behind him, wearing the print-goods dresses that he had designed and helped them make. Soldiers were searching thoroughly through the buildings.

"A low trick," he stated distinctly, though a trifle thickly, "unworthy of the noble antecedents of the Army of the United States! I had assumed, Colonel, that you were a gentleman!"

"Your assumptions, Doctor, contain little interest for me at this time!" said the colonel dryly. He sat his horse erectly, his soldierly austerity in no way lessened by the dust on his trim gray beard and in the creases of his weathered, aquiline face.

His cold piercing eyes played over Capi and Naka. He had on first sight touched his hat to them, taking them to be white girls, sisters, a charming pair in their matching dresses. Now he studied them and spoke of them to the doctor.

"Those girls are Indians."

"Civilized maids of Indian extraction," said

the doctor, his tone conveying lofty rebuke for crudeness.

"Why are they here?"

At certain stages of his drinking the doctor was apt to develop a facile inventiveness which, coupled with a convincing glibness, sometimes stood him in good stead and as often landed him in hot water.

"The young lady," he answered the colonel, emphasizing *lady,* "is my medical assistant. Very capable too, besides being a decorative asset to my office. The value of cheerful and pleasant surroundings for patients is recognized by leading medical authorities of Europe and—"

"We will forego the lecture," broke in the colonel.

Dr. Dwyer bowed. "As you wish, sir. I would not inflict knowledge where there obviously is a sufficiency. The little girl keeps house for me. Excellent cook. My duties require so much of my time and energy, I really—"

"Keep to the point, Doctor, if you please!" came the snappy request.

"I haven't lost it," retorted Dwyer. "The point is, as Mr. Colin DeBray's doctor I hold a pass from him to reside here within Sunrise boundaries. I believe that I have the right to choose the members of my own private and professional household. Correct me if I am mistaken."

"You are not mistaken." Colonel Buskirk kept looking at Capi and Naka. He frowned, as if casting back into memory. They had been muddy and in Indian garb when he saw them on the trail, and now they were fresh and dainty in their new dresses. Nor did they wear headbands, which made further difference.

They betrayed no sign of relief when he removed those probing eyes from them. The doctor had designed their dresses somewhat to ballroom style—full skirts and close-fitting bodices—and with their hands clasped modestly before them they stood for all the world like well-mannered white girls of good breeding, possibly Southern.

"However," pursued the colonel to Dwyer, "you must know that you're wanted for questioning."

"Officially, Colonel?"

"My order. For questioning in regard to your acquaintance with the Sioux shaman—who I now suspect to be the man I placed under arrest a few days ago. A white renegade or half-breed who called himself Hatch. He escaped. I received information that he probably was hiding here."

"Your information," Dr. Dwyer remarked, "came from neighbor Krahn of the Circle K, no doubt. It is incorrect, of course."

Colonel Buskirk made no response. He was looking toward the remainder of his detachment coming up from Despré herding a group of walking prisoners.

He returned the salute of the lieutenant when that officer approached him, and demanded, "These all?"

"All we could catch, sir," answered the lieutenant glumly, "and some of them claim to have passes. These people are as slippery as Apaches! They ghost off at sight of—"

"Never mind that," came the brusque interruption. Thc colonel, inspecting the prisoners as they shuffled to a standstill, fixed his eyes on one in particular, a tall man. "Lieutenant, I think you've captured a prize!" And raising his hand, finger pointing: "Bring that man here to me!"

Sam had the brim of his hat pulled down in front and his head bent, but he knew it was no good, and at the crisp command, "Bring that man here to me!" he lifted his head and looked straight into the colonel's eyes. Before a soldier could touch him he stepped out from among the scowling prisoners and stood before the colonel.

Saying nothing for a long time, a frown gathering on his severe countenance, the colonel finally barked, "Sergeant Wells!"

"Sir!" The sergeant touched his horse forward.

"Do you recognize this man? Look carefully!"

Sergeant Wells looked very carefully. He dismounted to peer into Sam's face, and that was his error, because at the arrest on Rush Creek he had not come to such close quarters with Sam and now Sam's surface bruises and lumps and cuts altered the contours of his features.

"You been in a brawl, man?" the sergeant murmured, and, receiving no reply, he stepped back and eyed Sam up and down and from side to side, much like a cattle buyer estimating beef weight on the hoof.

"It's his size, sir," he said. "And his eyes. But the rest of him—I dunno. He looks diff'rent. If Corporal Tuttle was here— He had more to do with—"

"*Private* Tuttle is on stable duty at Fort Reno," interposed the colonel correctingly. "Is this the man or isn't he?"

". . . I just dunno, sir, that's the truth."

"He looks a good deal like him to me!"

"Yessir. Me too. But—"

The colonel made an impatient gesture of dismissal to the sergeant and spoke directly to Sam. "Your name, business, where you're from, and how long have you been here?"

Sam went Indian, blanket Indian, mute and withdrawn. The apparent sullenness of captive Indian warriors, so exasperating to their white captors, was, as Sam knew, not sullenness at all. It represented a last act of stoic defiance. Any warrior at the end of his rope was likely to go blanket, showing no emotion whatsoever and cloaking himself in an impenetrable shroud of silence.

And, seeing the officer and the sergeant were not too sure of him, Sam made use of that frustrating trick. He simply stood there gazing before him, lips shut, his manner that of remote meditation having nothing to do with the urgent present.

It had its desired effect on Colonel Buskirk, whose brows drew together. “Won’t talk, eh?”

Dr. Dwyer inserted himself into it. “I’ll vouch for this man, Colonel,” he offered grandly. “My word on it, sir, he’s—”

“Quiet!” The single word, dry and biting, stopped him. “Give this man a horse and bring him on to Sunrise headquarters,” commanded the colonel. “Bring Dr. Dwyer along too.”

In the living room of the Sunrise ranch house Colonel Buskirk, curtly refusing a chair and a drink, cut directly to the offensive. His long and successful career as an army field officer was based on attack, always attack, and he carried that principle into practice in everything that he did, despising what was to him the deadening inactivity of desk work incumbent upon a post commander. As a veteran cavalryman he swore by the saddle as the proper seat of command, his backside boils regardless.

“You understand, Mr. DeBray, that it is

unlawful to harbor these people? Especially known criminals, fugitives?"

Colin DeBray nodded, his square face sagging from lassitude and a dull anxiety, but he countered heavily, "You can't hold me responsible for everybody who strays onto Sunrise range, Colonel."

"These people"—the colonel's tone dripped acid—"are hardly strays! They have been living within a mile of you, in that Despré rat nest!"

"My riders aren't paid to do police work. Known criminals and fugitives, you said. I don't know of any."

"Don't you, Mr. DeBray?" The colonel aimed a finger at Sam. "Don't you know who this man is? I think I do! He has changed his appearance since I arrested him at Rush Creek a few days ago, but I fancy he's my man!"

Tobe Overby had come into the house, and DeBray, looking to him to take up the anxious burden of somehow parrying the officer's charges, widened his lackluster eyes. This was the first today DeBray had seen of the Sunrise ramrod, and the fearfully battered face of the man surprised him hugely.

Overby caught the cue and took it up, drawling, "Sure we know him!"

Colonel Buskirk came full around with a level stare and, being new to the district, he demanded, "Who are you?" Then getting the prompt reply,

"I'm Overby, the foreman here," he nodded, and asked, "Well?"

And Tobe Overby, looking expressionlessly at Sam, said, "His name's Williams, and for a month now he's been breaking a bunch of broncs for Sunrise."

Amazed, wondering had he heard aright, Sam stared back incredulously at Overby, who took his eyes off him and looked steadily at DeBray. It simply wasn't possible, Sam thought, that this man who only a few hours ago had craved to kill him, then tried all out to cripple him, was now covering up for him with a barefaced lie.

As for Colonel Buskirk, he seemed to sway back slightly before uttering explosively, "A month! Here?"

"That's right," DeBray put in. "At two-fifty a head, isn't it, Tobe?"

"Yeah, and he's making money at it, more'n I'm making." The ramrod's voice contained the right amount of casual irony. "Better write him out a pass before his pockets get too hot."

Colonel Buskirk rounded on Sam. "Why is it you didn't tell me this? You refused to answer my questions!"

Sam shrugged. "My privilege," he murmured. A show of brash effrontery was fitting now, and he added blandly, "Thought I'd let you find it out from the heads for yourself, me being just dirt under your feet."

His face a study in angry bafflement, the colonel turned back to DeBray and rasped, "You're entirely too free with passes, Mr. DeBray, and I'm putting a stop to it! From the number of cattle you're running on this range, fifteen men should be sufficient crew. Cancel all passes above that number; any persons holding them will be picked up wherever found! Send the fifteen passes to Fort Reno for my signature."

DeBray sighed wearily, protesting, "The former commander never—"

"I am not guided by the actions of my predecessor," snapped the colonel. "This outfit has run things with a high hand in this part of the Territory, causing constant friction and trouble. Bad trouble! I remind you that you're here only on sufferance. And I may tell you that there's a strong movement afoot in Washington to clear out the whole bunch of you cattlemen and throw open all of Oklahoma for settlement!"

He was not done yet. He felt instinctively that he had been bamboozled, and he was cracking down on a troublemaking outfit that for far too long had flouted the army and made a travesty of law and order.

"Meantime," he wound up, "you will tear down every building here, every permanent structure, every fence! You have thirty days in which to carry out my orders, Mr. DeBray!"

"I reckon, Colin," remarked Overby, "it looks like we move into Despré."

"Despré is to be torn down too," said Colonel Buskirk relentlessly. "You'll have to live in tents as other outfits are doing."

With that he stalked out of the house, not bothering to take Dr. Dwyer along nor to pay Sam another glance. In a minute Sam left with Dwyer and, coming out, they saw the colonel riding off at the head of the cavalry detachment and prisoners. They had been brought here on army horses; but the animals were in the detachment, so Sam and Dwyer started their tramp on foot back to the stage station, when Overby came out onto the porch and hailed them.

"Borrow a couple jugheads. Turn 'em loose there, they'll drift back." And to Sam, tonelessly: "You're a Sunrise man now. Don't wander off the reservation, or the soldiers will pick you up."

Going back into the living room, Overby said softly, "Phew, that was close!" He watched Colin DeBray half fill a tumbler with whisky at the sideboard, eying him wryly. "If they'd taken Hatch to Fort Reno . . ." Slapping his hands together, he flared the open palms upward, mimicking explosion. "Boom! Good night all!"

DeBray, glass in hand, swung around from the sideboard. "It's good night anyway," he muttered huskily. Gulping down a good half of the whisky, he blew a breath and went on, "All this, my house, everything . . . And if they throw the country open to settlers that's the end of it. Everything's breaking up."

Overby shrugged. "I looked for it to come sooner or later. Not this soon, but sometime. Nothing lasts forever. We've had a good ride here. Still got the cattle, a hell of a sight more'n we started with. And about a thousand head of horses. Money in the sack. We'll have a good ride some other place." He was thinking while he spoke, *I will, anyhow.*

DeBray shook his head, sinking into the nearest chair with an old man's low grunt. "It's not for me, Tobe. Move on to new range? Leave here and build again? God, no!"

Not for you, no, Overby thought. *For me.* And enjoying his own double play, his secret, he said, "Aw, you'll face up to it when the time comes, Colin." He was about to get a drink for himself, and a thought struck him. "I wonder," he muttered, "what Hatch thinks about me covering for him?"

At that minute Sam was saying, more to himself than to Dwyer, "Why did he do it? Last night he tried to kill me. And that was his second try, I'm pretty sure. We fought, and I beat the living daylights out of him. You saw his face."

"I can see yours too. Not pretty, either of you."

"And now," Sam pursued, "he pulls me out of a jack pot like that! Why?"

The doctor didn't care much why and said idly, "Perhaps the fight settled things between you."

"Not on your life!"

"Well, I didn't actually think so," Dwyer admitted. "Wasn't thinking. Need a drink. That devil chills my blood."

THIRTEEN

The Sunrise roundup crew on East Ten pasture was full-handed, and the crew boss, Red Fane, showed his surprise when Tobe Overby, immediately on riding into camp, took him aside and stated, "I'm sending all hands out to you, Red, the cook included."

"I don't need 'em. We're pretty well caught up now."

"You'll need 'em. We're moving—lock, stock, and barrel!"

"Movin'?" Red Fane stared. "You mean Sunrise is—?"

"Sunrise is all through here." Overby put into his voice a bitterness he did not feel. "Colonel Buskirk's orders, damn him! We throw our herds together and start tonight by the moon. You'll be in charge of thc start, Red."

The responsibility and the short notice caused Red to blink. "That's one hell of a big trail herd to handle!"

Overby shrugged off the objection. "Old John Chisum drove ten thousand head from Concho to the Pecos in '67. What anybody else can do, we can do. You'll have enough men."

"I been wondering why you've had us hold the herds so close," Red said. "At that we'll be missin' a lot o' stuff that ain't gathered yet."

"Can't be helped. We'll more than make it up from Circle K."

Red came alert. "How's that?"

Knowing this man well, Overby said freely, "I'll be taking the Despré bunch on a Circle K raid tonight. Outside of Whiteside and three or four others, the soldiers caught mostly the sodbusters. It rids us of deadwood. The rest can't last long with Sunrise gone. This is their chance to get out with a stake. We'll burn Krahn out, stampede his horses, and drive off every Circle K critter we find!"

Pursing his lips in a low whistle, Red muttered in awe, "A clean sweep for farewell!" And then: "Wait a minute! Soon's they catch up horses, they'll come at Sunrise sure, and nobody'll be there! They'll—"

"That's right," Overby broke in. "Nobody there for 'em to nail. They'll burn the layout. It's to be torn down anyhow. Save us the job."

"They'll be hot on your trail, maybe with law!"

"Right again. So what you do, Red, is follow right over our tracks with the Sunrise herd. I'll drop back to you and let the bunch push on ahead with the Circle K stuff. When Circle K catches up we beat 'em off. If they've got law with 'em—well, we're driving Sunrise cattle, is all."

Red grinned. "And no tracks left of their stuff! Yeah, I'll make sure o' that! What's the route?"

"Same the boys have used before, taking out Circle K stuff. Up to the North Canadian and west through the Cherokee Strip, into New Mexico. We sell off Krahn's cattle there where we've sold 'em before, for what they'll bring. Sunrise, though, pushes on."

"To where?" Red asked, and was made curious by Overby's fleeting thin smile.

"There's good range open up toward the northwest corner of New Mexico," Overby said, "near the Divide. It'll be Sunrise range when we get there."

"Mountain country," Red commented, not too happy about it. "Can the Old Man"—meaning DeBray—"make such a trip?"

"Says he can," Overby lied. What he privately proposed doing with DeBray not even Red Fane would willingly countenance, for it outraged the code of the most conscienceless cowmen. "And . . . Miss Victoria too."

"She comin'?" Red was sincerely startled. "That country's plain wild an' mighty lonesome! I been there."

Overby nodded, stepping to his waiting horse and lifting toe to stirrup. "So've I. Mighty lonesome. It'll do fine."

Now that he had set things rolling, Overby had a final bit of business at the Sunrise layout to look into. It was something that he was practically certain of in his mind, but he needed to be positive of it. There could be no slip-up at this stage.

Unusual for him, Colin DeBray sat on the front porch in a cowhide chair, gazing out beyond the yard. For months he had kept indoors, sunk in the apathy that gripped his spirit. It was years since he had been on a horse.

He nodded to the ramrod drawing up at the house, and, shortening his faraway gaze, he queried, "Where's everybody? Place is deserted as a graveyard."

The simile was so unconsciously apt that Tobe Overby had to repress a smile. "Roundup hit a snag, and I had to send all hands to help," he replied easily. "Maria back?"

DeBray shook his head. His Mexican housekeeper was still off at her sister's cabin, he said, helping to take care of her sister's sick children. "She sent a boy here with word the kids are worse. Victoria's gone to get Dr. Dwyer for 'em."

"Oh? I don't know why she should trouble herself." Overby stepped onto the porch and sat on the railing, swinging one leg. He had his words lined up, and he said, "I've been thinking. As you know, I've been able to soak away some money here, like you. What if I got killed? A man's got to die some time. I'd like to leave it to Victoria. How would I go about that, Colin?"

DeBray regarded him with surprise. "Victoria won't hardly need it, but if you want to—well, just make out your will."

"Is that what you've done?" Then snapping his long fingers: "I forgot. You don't need to, she being your only kin."

"Don't need to, maybe," DeBray said, "but I've done it to make sure. A St. Louis law firm has got my will on file. Victoria knows about it. She gets everything. And I've fixed it so she can draw my money from the St. Louis bank any time."

Some sort of presentiment brought a flicker of animation into his heavily listless face, and he stopped, then asked, "Why did you want to know . . ."

But Overby, vaulting the porch railing and dropping to the ground with the effortless agility of a cat, was saying across the Sunrise owner's words, "Guess I'll mosey to Despré and see what we can salvage before it's torn down." He took to saddle and made off.

Left alone once more on the layout, DeBray sat plucking at his lower lip. Going over the ramrod's questions, he felt that they had been bent to a hidden motive. The feeling grew, taking on sinister undercurrents. Twenty years of indirect blackmailing by Overby had left DeBray without any trust whatever in the man.

He rose, grunting, and tramped inside, hideously worried. The silent house was like a tomb to him all of a sudden, and it came to him that he was helpless, old, really alone. There was nobody to turn to.

The condition of Overby's face meant that he had fought with somebody and been bested. Hatch? DeBray reverted to his half-formed hope that Overby would tangle with Hatch and that Hatch would kill him. It had not transpired. DeBray sighed deeply. Nothing worked out for him any more. Nobody to turn to. Nobody at all.

Victoria rode the all-white mare, the same animal on which Sam had first seen her. She wore a brocaded dress of heavy green silk—uncommon apparel for cow country, but green was her preferred color, and she knew perfectly well that she looked at her vivid best in it. And besides, nonconformity, particularly in dress, filled to some measure the need to express her individuality and release herself from the cramping dictates of conventional decorum. The skirt necessitated use of the sidesaddle, and that showed off an accomplished horsewoman to advantage.

Coming out of the stage station to greet her, Sam experienced a certain little difficulty in controlling his voice and eyes. With her full-formed beauty to enchant the senses, Victoria could cause any hale man to catch his breath and entertain instant visions. Her feminine intuition fathomed to its depth the tall man's reaction, and her ice-green eyes flashed dazzlingly before she prudently lowered their lashes.

They exchanged meaningless phrases of greeting after which Victoria spoke of Maria's message that her sister's sick children had taken a turn for the worse. "I came to ask Dr. Dwyer to go to them," Victoria said, conscious that good Samaritanism formed only part of her motive for coming here.

"The doctor is—out of action just now," Sam told her. Dwyer had managed to cop a jug from the derelict Lucky Jack ahcad of the Despré men returning from hiding. He was stone drunk.

Victoria had heard of the doctor's fatal weakness and, realizing Sam's meaning, she shaped her mouth in a soundless "Oh" of regret.

"The boy said the children's throats are inflamed and they're gasping for breath. It sounds like diphtheria, doesn't it?"

Sam was unfamiliar with that medical term. The symptoms were those of what Mexicans called *el garrotillo*, the strangler, dreadcd killer of children.

"Could *you* help them, Sam?" Victoria asked him, and he nodded, his thoughts going to the old painted parfleche that so often had plunged him into trouble, making an outcast of him and finally a hunted fugitive.

"I can try," he said, "if they're not too far gone."

"I'll go with you," she volunteered.

"It's dangerous," he warned her. "People catch it easily from the sick."

"I've had diphtheria. It never strikes a person twice. You need me, Sam, if only to show you the way to the cabin."

"True. All right, I'll get my horse. We'll have to stop by where I've hidden the wagon and pick up the parfleche."

From an open window of the station Capi watched them depart. She had been witness to their interchange of looks, their expressions, their eyes. Their conversation, however, had not reached her, and she knew nothing of their destination. There they went, riding off side by side, together again, Sam and the gold-and-white woman.

Capi rested her forehead on the window sill and could not hold back any longer the slow, scalding tears.

Compared to Sunrise, Krahn's Circle K outfit was a late-comer to the Territory, and in grudging compliance with federal orders its headquarters consisted of an array of temporary tent shacks, half lumber and half canvas, from a distance resembling a small army post. The only square of yellow lamplight came from the tent shack that served as Krahn's ranch office.

Krahn, working late and in a foul temper because the tally books showed shortages, stepped outside and listened, frowning. In the hush, he heard the ordinary sounds of the layout, occasional movements of horses in the corrals, the snoring of men asleep in the tent shacks. But something else was steadily intruding, a murmur of sound that traveled through the earth, and this was what had fetched him out. He made it to be a muffled pounding somewhere off in the moonlit night.

A figure moved toward him, and from it issued the muted voice of his foreman, Henry Butler: "You hear it too, boss?" Henry was in his long gray underwear, boots, and hat, but wide awake. "I thought I was dreamin' it, an' then—"

Krahn motioned him quiet. "Coming closer." Presently he said, "It's stopped now."

"What the hell?" Henry muttered. "Can't be any the night crew comin' off herd guard. You reckon it's some outfit night-owlin' through? Or soldiers, maybe?"

Krahn snapped, "Rouse the men out! We'll go see—" And he was turning to his office when the pounding started up again with a roar. A single shot cracked, and all at once horsemen came plunging headlong down the ridge that sheltered the layout from north gales.

Krahn bellowed an oath and jumped inside for a rifle, and Henry Butler, who had come out unarmed, streaked to his tent shack, shouting for the men. A volley of gunfire followed the single shot, livid spurts licking out from the descending riders, now raising high-pitched squalls.

In seconds all was confusion; Circle K men tumbling out half-dressed, and excited horses erupting a wild racket in the corrals. The riders, shooting and yelling, struck the layout and swept on through, their excitement-mad horses bowling men over in the dirt. Krahn, lunging forth with a rifle, almost stepped into the path of a horseman swirling by and took a boot in the chest. He crashed back into the door of his office and tore it off its hinges, knocking the whole front of the tent shack askew.

Scrambling up and out again, Krahn bawled stridently, “The horses!” and got off a shot after the riders. But he knew with raging dismay that nothing he or his men could do was going to stop disaster.

Through the yelling and gunfire came the noisy smashing of corral fences and then the thunder of the horse herd stampeding in panic. The riders, heading the animals off to a flying start, swung clear and raced on southeast in a bobbing bunch, soon vanishing over the next ridge. The swift raid, executed in the space of a minute, was complete.

From off to Krahn’s left Henry Butler called, “Boss, you all right?” and limped to him. Some of the Circle K men had got banged up, and Henry himself had a hurt ankle. “They was Sunrisers,” he said, and loosed a stream of obscenities. “I don’t think we put a scratch on ’em!”

Krahn was trying to contain his rage. “Get your

clothes and guns, everybody!" he rasped. "We're going after our horses before the moon's down. When we catch up enough to ride, we're going after Sunrise! Hop to it!"

They tried to hurry, but injuries slowed some of them, and it took Krahn and his foreman some time to get them started out in the direction that the horse herd had taken. There wasn't a horse left on the layout, and they had to go it afoot, an intolerable and painful outrage to saddle men wearing tight boots with high heels that sank into the soil at every step. Cursing fervidly, they tramped after Krahn, making slow progress.

They had gone hardly a mile when one in the rear exclaimed, "Hey, do I hear 'em comin' back?" and that brought them to halt, tensely listening, fingering their rifles.

There was the pounding again, steadily swelling in volume, but this was different, much heavier and having a rolling cadence like that of a thousand bass drums. Very soon it gained a moaning overtone, split by thin yells.

"That's cattle!" the man sang out, voicing a fact that now was plain to all of them. "They're a-boilin' straight this way!"

"Ridge!" Krahn broke into a run, his men slogging behind him. To be caught on foot in a cattle stampede was death, and they forgot their injuries, clambering and clawing up the steep slope of the nearest ridge.

Just below the rocky outcrop topping the crest, they stopped to look back. They could see the rippling swarm of cattle now in the moonlight, coming like a dark wave—Circle K cattle, the whole beef herd, driven on the rampage—and, foreseeing catastrophe, Henry Butler cried hoarsely, "Oh Christ, no! No—!" But Krahn, his face contorted in a fixed wince, didn't let out a sound.

One minute the Circle K layout was standing, a group of pale squares and oblongs, and the next minute it was demolished, the flimsy tent shacks collapsing under the close-packed onrush of cattle. The herd rushed on, bawling, deafening, fragments of canvas fluttering from horns, broken sections of plank side walls tossed and borne along like flotsam. A whooping rider dashed with drunken recklessness close along the left flank of the storming mass and was gone before any of the Circle K watchers on the ridge could snap a shot down at him.

Then the herd had swarmed on, leaving a flattened scatter of debris, and Henry Butler was groaning numbly, "Wrecked our layout with our own beef herd, by God! Wrecked it to hell—!"

The men said nothing, shocked to speechless fury. All they had left was the clothes they stood in and the saddles they had lugged with them. In a little while Krahn said in a voice that was strangely quiet for him, "Let's get after those horses."

FOURTEEN

Tobe Overby got back alone to Sunrise as the eastern sky was lifting toward dawn and, avoiding the house, he rode on around to the barn. The departing Sunrise crew had emptied the corrals, by his order leaving him his tall sorrel and a team for the buckboard. The animals stood in closed stalls, ready for him to use.

The black horse was worn out from the night's work, for he had done much hard riding and used it harshly. Backing the sorrel out of its stall, he transferred saddle and bridle to it. His intention was to harness the team and tie the sorrel to lead behind the buckboard, making everything ready before taking the next and final step, but a fierce impatience seized him and, stepping to the open barn door, he stared with smoldering eyes at the house.

The night's work was done, and well done, as smooth as could be. Under his leadership the Despré hard cases had smashed Krahn's Circle K and were roaring northwest right now with the Circle K beef herd. He had ridden back then and checked to see for himself that Red Fane and the crew were driving the mammoth Sunrise trail herd on the course of the stolen herd and obliterating its tracks.

All he needed now to satisfy any questions that would eventually arise was legal title to the Sunrise brand. Or what amounted to the same thing, control of title. Iron control. He knew exactly how he was going to go about obtaining that.

And should the Despré bunch meet up with trouble before reaching the New Mexico market—law officers, soldiers, cattle inspectors, or the like—well, that was their lookout. Nobody could hang that steal on Tobe Overby, boss of Sunrise, a rich outfit on the move to new range. He had everything cinched down from all angles.

By its very silence, its vulnerable aloneness, the house drew Overby to walk soundlessly toward it. Irresistible, its total lack of protection against him. The crew would not be back, ever. They believed that the DeBrays were packing up to follow them. Krahn and his tough hands, bent on vengeance, could not get here for hours yet, having first to catch up horses to ride.

"Get on with it!" he murmured. "Nobody around for miles—" The thought of Sam Hatch came to him. A mile and quarter to the old stage station.

"Got to fix that joker! Can do it before I leave. Just drop by, say a word or two to throw him off, and—"

He found that he was breathing faster as he approached the house. It annoyed him as a kind of unexpected weakness in himself, and to combat it he brought forward in full his ingrained cruelty, his lust for inflicting injury and pain.

He stepped onto the front porch. The front door was never locked and, ghost-quiet, he opened it and entered, closing it behind him. The lifting sky provided enough gray light through the windows for him to find his way, and he was familiar with the house and the placement of furniture.

Pondering for a few seconds at Victoria's door, he passed on to Colin DeBray's room on the other side of the house. He opened the door and looked in.

Colin DeBray lay fast asleep under the bed-covers. Overby took note of the medicine bottle on the bedside table. It was about a third empty, and he smiled. Colin's idea of a teaspoon dose was a straight slug from the bottle. Overby slid his gun out, tilting it at the motionless shape, then shook his head slightly.

"Let's not take a chance on it! Let Circle K do it, me long gone! A shot now— No."

Retracing his silent steps to Victoria's door, he paused outside it to consider the spot where, in case it was locked, he would hit it with his shoulder and burst it open. He was breathing fast again, almost panting, but now he bared his teeth in a grin at himself, knowing that his nerve was unaffected, and he laid a perfectly steady hand on the doorknob and softly turned it.

The door was unlocked. He eased it open, while in back of his mind a cool thought ran: "I was this quiet before, and she got away from me. Not this time. She can't—"

He pushed the door wide and moved in swiftly, hands before him, long fingers spread. Then he was staring in furious disbelief.

The bed, neatly made up, not a wrinkle showing, was empty. It had not been slept in.

A minute later Overby was spurring out of the barn, growling incoherently, hell-bent for the stage station.

Despré stood deserted in the spreading dawn. Its furtive denizens had learned of Colonel Buskirk's stringent orders that the abandoned old trail town was to be torn down. That, and the fact that Sunrise was moving out, left them bereft of any further prospects here. They had all decamped with the stolen Circle K beef herd, in hopes of a stake to set them up elsewhere.

It was the sight of the Lucky Jack, a reminder that Hatch was fast and dangerous, that restored to Overby his sense of discretion, and he drew to a halt to put his thoughts in order.

To go stamping all primed up to the stage station would give Hatch instant warning. From his looks, Hatch had survived many a wicked fight and knew too well how to take care of himself. Overby swung down off his tall sorrel.

Daylight advanced swiftly now, and he looked all around to see that he was unobserved.

From his saddle pocket he took out a snub-nosed pistol, an extra weapon that he carried for emergencies. It was a .41 caliber five-shot, with the handle rounded and trigger guard removed, and its holster was cut down to a minimum and attached flat to a thin leather belt. Opening his shirt, Overby fitted it carefully around his middle, next to his skin, tucking holster and gun under his waistband on the left side. This simple rig was better, he had found, than any shoulder holster. A pretense of absently scratching your belly or hoisting your pants . . .

Remounting, he deliberately quelled his inner ferment and made his face slack. He held the sorrel to a trot the rest of the way, arriving at the stage station with the easy and unhurried mien of a man whose purpose was in no manner pressing.

"Hatch?" Even his tone he kept casual. "DeBray wants you."

Waiting for response, he legged down, yawning. He heard nothing and stepped to the doorway and looked in, repeating, "Hatch?"

Still no sound. He entered and went through the rooms. They were vacant and, coming out in a state of controlled frenzy, he struck across the yard to the harness shed and flung open the door. Dr. Dwyer lay stretched face down on his bunk, a blanket over him, breathing hard through his open mouth. Capi and Naka sat silently together at the foot of the bunk, watching over him.

Overby grasped the short beard and ungently twisted the doctor's head around. "Dead drunk! Then he couldn't have gone with her to—"

He swung glaring on the two girls. "Hatch and Victoria DeBray—d'you know where they are?"

They looked at him, their eyes veiled, knowing him for an enemy, reading violence in the gaunt, sin-ravaged visage. "No," said Capi.

Sensing that she told the truth, Overby nevertheless cast off the surface restraint that he had been clamping upon himself and loosed his savage anger at her, snarling, "You wouldn't tell me if you did know, damn you! Didn't they get back all night?"

"No."

He cuffed her heavily in the face, sending her to the floor. Naka swiftly knelt beside her. They didn't utter a sound, watching him. His rage took a low tangent, and he considered the girl on the floor. She was young and shapely, stirringly desirable. At any other time . . .

He cursed, quitting the shed. That was it, he was pushed for time. Krahn and the Circle K men would be swooping down on Sunrise today. This morning. Maybe within the hour. Last night's stampeding of their horses had left them afoot, but not forever. In that size bunch of horses there were bound to be a few placid jugheads that would stand to be caught without much fuss, and catching others thereafter from the saddle was no trouble.

His virulent cursing scared the sorrel to dancing, and he wrenched the reins brutally. He should have been on his way by now, with Victoria—broken to bridle like a horse.

All was smoothly in operation, and Victoria was missing, thc Sunrisc hciress, key to the whole move. That was the unforeseen snag. Overby knew the location of the Mexican cabin. He contemplated going to it.

But that would take up time. Again that cursed matter of time! And there was no guarantee that he would find Victoria and Hatch at the cabin. If that was where they had spent the night tending to some sick Mexican brats—and to Overby that was by no means a certainty—by now they most likely had left. Nor could he, if he started out, be sure of meeting them. There were half a dozen different routes to that cabin. They could have reached Sunrise while he was wasting precious time at the stage station.

At that thought Overby started back to the layout as fast as he had raced from it, but in his raging temper he did not discard preparedness. He left open a bottom button of his shirt and slid his right hand into the gap a few times as he rode, polishing up his reach for the hide-out .41 five-shot.

• • •

They had stayed up all night with the sick children in the cabin of Maria's sister, a widow. *El garrotillo*—diphtheria—was what it was, requiring all of Sam's skill and knowledge of herbs to combat the child-killer. Four of the five children, he believed, were safely through the worst of it, but, for the youngest one, he held little hope, and that depressed him. Tall Horse would have done better, and probably Dr. Dwyer might have too. Sam felt himself to be inadequate, a second-rate shaman. Maybe—the wry thought did not amuse him—he should have tried some incantations and mesmerism on that puny littlest one.

Sam busied himself packing the parfleche into the wagon among the rest of the telltale Indian belongings. Covering the load with the canvas that had served as a wagon top, he weighted it down with rocks to prevent its being blown off by wind, and over it he spread brush and branches to help keep it hidden.

Finishing this task, he backed out of the wagon and jumped down off the tail gate to find Victoria leaning back against the off rear wheel of the wagon, half-reclining on it, and stretching her arms luxuriantly.

"Such a lovely, lovely dawn!" she said.

The rising sun balanced on the horizon. Standing by the bay horse, Sam glanced toward it.

About this time Dwyer would either be swearing off or refortifying himself from the jug. Capi and Naka would be fixing breakfast. Sam waited for Victoria to indicate a readiness to leave.

She evinced no such inclination at the moment, asking him, "Is it true, Sam, that Indians sing to the morning sun?"

"Some do. Sometimes."

"I'd love to hear it."

"To your ears it would not sound musical."

As if his words contained no meaning or were not reaching her, she said softly, "Sing it to me, Sam, before we go on."

He would have refused curtly had she been anything of an Indian-hater or, worse, displayed the slightest trace of a patronizing attitude. As it was, he mentally shrugged. If it would get them on their way . . .

He called to mind a Cheyenne song of offering sung at sunrise. A simple thing; its significance, a form of spiritual purification. A mental image came to him, from boyhood, of a visiting Cheyenne chief in a Sioux *hocoka*, arms upraised, singing it as the sun appeared.

> "*E-ya ha we ye . . . he ye ye*!
> *He ye ho*! *We ye . . . whi ye ye . . .*"

Sam sang quietly—a chant in three or four notes was what it was, really—with his gaze automatically turned to the east, above and beyond Victoria's shining hair.

"*E-ya ha we ye . . . he ye ye*!
He ye ho! *We ye . . . hai i-yi hi ha* . . . !"

At first without much expression, his voice began gaining sonorous depth and emphasis, with rhythmical pulsation on sustained notes. His gaze shortened to Victoria.

Captured by the repetition and tempo, she was swaying her golden head slightly. Her ice-green eyes, fixed unblinkingly on his, glistened brilliantly. A glow lighted up her face like a hot blush, and her breasts rose, and her vibrant aliveness was a passion as visible as flame. And then Sam was singing the song of offering, not to the rising sun but to her, his direct gaze fusing with hers.

Victoria spread her arms back along the iron rim of the wagon wheel, resting her head against the side of the wagon.

She said strangely, "I have never been alive. Not truly alive. Something . . ." She paused. Her muted voice was not her own. It was husky and all but toneless as she went on: "Something inside me. A cold hand. Worse than chains. It has held me back against my will. I've been a prisoner, half-alive. A walking shell of a woman—a nothing. . . ."

She said in a changed voice, "I am alive now. Truly alive. I'm free . . . !"

Sam turned his head. He would not let his eyes go to her, would not trust himself. Alive? She was vibrant with life. Puritanical austerity had no part or place in Sam's make-up. Despite his shaman background of rigorous reserve and reticence, by nature he was essentially an outgoing man. But he was served now by instinct and by a reaction that he could not easily define or explain. And so he stood impassive as Victoria spoke again.

"I am a woman now! A whole and complete woman! Sam . . . !"

His intentional unresponsiveness then getting through to her, she tilted her head to look at him, first with wondering and next with shocked dismay. She had thrown aside that pride of hers and revealed herself as a woman desperate for love, unashamedly in surrender, vulnerable to his slightest advance; and he was simply rejecting her as she had rejected many men.

That he had allowed her to fall into intolerable embarrassment, had delivered to her the unforgivable affront, he realized keenly. He hoped she would be angry rather than crushed, and when her anger did come he was relieved. Although her anger was turned upon herself, it was a healthy reaction.

"I—I've made a fool of myself!" she murmured shakily, stiff-lipped. Her hands clenched tightly on the rim of the wagon wheel. “When a woman goes to reckless lengths deliberately and finds— Oh!” In angry detestation of the touch of the wagon she stepped abruptly away from it and, standing erect with head high and cheeks flaming, she said an extraordinary thing:

“Desperation! It was well named! Nothing ever really prospers here! There’s a curse on this land!”

It brought Sam’s eyes to her. “What?” he exclaimed. “What was that?”

From his confused memory of early boyhood before the massacre and his mind-clouded wanderings, the persistent recollection recurred to him of his father saying: *“We’re going north to a place called Desperation. . . .”*

He forced his voice to a quiet pitch, asking Victoria the question whose answer stood good to lead him onto a twenty-year-old trail: “Desperation? You know of such a place? Where?” Suddenly he had the feel of approaching closely to the brink of discovery, for other long-forgotten memories were arising, taking on recognizable shape like old acquaintances coming through darkness.

Deep in her angry embarrassment and perhaps thankful to change the subject, Victoria replied, “Here. People were calling it that when I was a little girl. The promised stage road had failed to come through, so the stage station, Despré’s

Station, failed, and some humorist called it Desperation."

"I should've thought of that!" Sam muttered. His mouth was dry. Memories were rushing at him now. Scenes, voices, his father speaking again . . .

"And then the town," Victoria said. "The trail herds went another route. Despré, too, became known as Desperation. And the range, during a long drought—Desperation Range. A land of desperate failure! My father changed it after he came up from Texas and established Sunrise here. He hated the name. He'd fire a man he heard using it. After a while people dropped it."

". . . A place called Desperation." John Heward's voice reached across the span of twenty years. *"Yes, we're leasing it. . . ."*

Victoria moved on to the white mare and gathered up the reins. She said, "But my father has never been happy here. He and my mother broke up. I only come back to—well, it's mostly a sort of duty to him."

"This new foreman I'm hiring to head the outfit up 'pears to be a mighty good man." It was like listening to the voice of a ghost. *"Married man. Got a little daughter. Our Sam won't take much to that, I reckon, but Sis . . ."*

"He's lonely, and he's aging terribly fast."

"His name is . . ."

"The DeBrays are not a happy family."

". . . Spells it with a big B in the middle . . ."

"We have money, but—" Victoria never finished. A sound from Sam brought her about, in the act of mounting onto the sidesaddle. "What's the matter?"

Sam, expelling pent-up breath in a growling sigh, had slapped the flank of the bay horse and was vaulting aboard like an Indian brave in a hurry. Victoria shrank from the look on his face.

"Sam—!"

Wordlessly he shook his head and put the bay to a run down the arroyo, and Victoria rode the mare after him, bewildered and fearful.

FIFTEEN

Tobe Overby rode the tall sorrel on into the barn after a careful survey of the Sunrise layout. He saw no signs of any visitors during his absence nor anything to show that Victoria had returned, with or without Sam Hatch, and, lifting his rifle from its saddle boot, he walked with it over to the house.

He strode in to find Colin DeBray drinking hot coffee in the kitchen. The Sunrise owner had made the coffee himself, there being nobody around this morning to do it for him. He was drinking it black, laced with whisky to pull him out of the fog of drugged sleep, and over the cup he shot his thick eyebrows up in perfunctory greeting to the ramrod.

Not troubling to return the nod, Overby demanded, "Didn't she get back yet?"

"Who—Maria? I told her she could stay with her sister till the kids are better."

"Hell, no, I mean Victoria! She's been gone all night and now it's—" Overby checked himself, shaking his head curtly to DeBray's gesture toward the coffeepot on the table.

"She's there helping out too. Sent the Mexican boy to tell me she wouldn't be back till this morning. Dr. Dwyer—"

“The doc’s not there! He’s on a drunk!”

“Oh?” DeBray sloshed more whisky into his cup and added coffee. He drank reflectively, eying Overby, becoming aware of the man’s hurried air, and noticing the rifle. “What’s that for?”

“Fixing to clean it.”

“How’s the work coming along?”

“Fine.”

Another question plucked for attention in DeBray’s rising consciousness, and as it took final shape he put the cup down and sat up straight, asking, “How did you know Victoria wasn’t home last night?”

“You told me yesterday she’d gone to get the doc,” Overby reminded him.

DeBray nodded. “Sure. She could’ve come back, though, while you were gone. You haven’t been here all night yourself. Or have you? I slept heavy. I wouldn’t have heard you.”

Thumping the butt of the rifle noisily on the floor, Overby inquired, “What are you getting at, Colin? I stayed the night at roundup camp.”

“You did, huh?” DeBray met the leaden stare. “Then how the hell did you know my daughter didn’t spend the night in her room? Tell me that!”

“Guessed it.” Overby could think of no better reply and didn’t much care. His plans were going through, and their conclusion was too close in view for him to bother with contriving further subtleties.

DeBray did not let his gaze waver. “Tobe,” he said, “I think that’s a damn lie! What’re you up to?”

A rage of impatience seized Tobe Overby, and suddenly he had had enough of this. On the instant, he slung the rifle up in both hands, waist-high, muzzle leveled across the kitchen table at DeBray’s startled face.

“All right!” he rasped. A wild exultation rang in his voice, a savage glee at coming right out with a statement of intention and hurling it at the victim. “All right, I’ll tell you! I’m taking Sunrise over! The whole outfit’s on the move, miles off and going strong!”

DeBray turned gray, sitting motionless, his hands on the table. Presently he moved stiffened lips to say, “I’m the registered owner of the Sunrise brand. D’you figure to kill me?”

Overby’s eyes mocked him. “I’m leaving that to Circle K. We raided ’em last night. They ought to be here pretty soon.”

“You can’t get away with this, Tobe,” DeBray said flatly. “When I’m dead, Victoria automatically becomes owner.”

Overby nodded. “And she’ll be with the outfit.” His gaunt features creased in a smile, saturninely cruel. “She’ll sure make an obedient wife, I guarantee, by the time we—” Then as

DeBray, who didn't carry a gun on him, reached a hand toward the coffeepot Overby rapped out: "Leave that be!"

DeBray didn't leave it. His square face a block of grimness, he caught up the coffeepot by its handle to fling the scalding contents at the renegade ramrod. Before he could complete the action, Overby whipped the rifle forward in an arc and struck him over the temple with the barrel. As DeBray rocked sideways from the stunning blow, Overby hit him again, viciously. DeBray and the chair crashed to the floor, coffee and grounds spilling everywhere.

"Damn fool!" Overby kicked the senseless man and, getting no reaction, he left him lying there and hurried through to the front of the house.

The raging impatience was tightening up in him. Time was running out, and he had to be on his way before the Circle K crew rampaged along, primed to retaliate for last night's devastating raid; but to leave without Victoria would put a fatal crimp in his plans. Cursing, his whole body taut with urgency, he glared out through an open front window. The sun was climbing well above the horizon. What if she wasn't coming home till noon?

He would have to go to the cabin, hiding the buckboard and team somewhere along the way, and get in his shot at Hatch at the first opportunity. If Hatch and Victoria were not still there . . .

Overby made himself stop thinking along that line, because it had no profit, but anxiety and fury tore at his insides. He was starting for the door when he saw something that pulled him up short. Two riders, one ahead of the other, were riding fast down the Despré road leading here to the layout. They were too far off to be recognized, and for a moment their headlong gait persuaded him that they might be forerunners of the Circle K avengers.

But then he caught the flash of the all-white mare in the sun, and a little later the color of the bay horse. He was able then to batten down his inner tumult and, taking post at the open window, he knelt and laid the barrel of the rifle on the sill in readiness.

"Come on!" he muttered. "Come and get it, joker!"

Where the road dipped behind a low rise the two riders momentarily vanished. A better thought for ambush made Overby get up off his knees and place a chair five feet from the window, its back toward it. Straddling the chair and using its back as a rest for his elbows, Overby cradled the rifle.

"Might's well be comfortable."

He had clear and unobstructed view of the gate to the yard and of the road running from it to the house. This position couldn't be bettered, as he found by sighting experimentally at a stone on the road. And this far back from the window, the rifle would not catch any telltale glint of sunshine along the barrel.

"Ready for you, Mr. Hatch!"

The two riders reappeared, and shortly they swung in through the gate, Hatch first, then Victoria, coming straight up toward the house.

Overby took aim, getting Hatch dead in line with his sights. But, swearing softly, he held his fire for a few seconds longer, because Victoria was riding directly behind Hatch and there was risk of a through-and-through bullet hitting her.

Waiting for them to swerve apart, Overby wondered at the reason for such hard riding. And in those few seconds his ears caught two small noises in the room behind him: a brushing sound and a lean click. He twisted his head around sharply.

Colin DeBray leaned, sagging, against the frame of the door that led to the kitchen, his hair and face blood-clotted. His eyes were fastened on Overby's back. He was using both hands to raise a cocked gun, a .44 single-action that Overby recognized as one that DeBray used to wear before he quit the saddle.

With perhaps half a second between life and death Overby hurled himself around, sending the chair flying out from under him, and fired the rifle. Legs astride, he watched DeBray topple away from the doorframe, snarled, "Damn you!" and whirled back to the window.

The two riders had separated.

Hearing the shot and the crash of the chair inside the house, Sam instantly veered off his course, calling, "Watch out!" to Victoria behind him, although with no idea that she might be in any danger except from an accidental bullet.

He was conditioned by his thinking to believe that the shot had been fired at him. It brought to him a measure of caution that he needed, and so he bent low in the saddle and raced to the near end of the double bunkhouse.

A hasty rifleshot ripped after him. It screeched overhead. Then he was rounding the bunkhouse corner, all but scraping it, and riding along the building's rear. At the far end he dropped off the bay, sliding his rifle, dead Manuelito's stolen Winchester, from its saddle boot. He peered out.

From this angle of vision he could see only the back of the house. Victoria was not in sight. Sam guessed that she must have ridden on to the front of the house and dismounted and run on in. Speed in attack was Sam's inclination, and he sprinted on foot across the bare expanse of yard. Reaching the back door, he heard a small cry, a woman's sobbing cry. He pushed the door open and went in.

He was in the kitchen, seeing an overturned

chair and a spilled coffeepot on the floor, hearing sounds from the living room. He prowled forward.

Two short hallways ran from the kitchen to the living room, for this house, although not overly large for an outfit the size of Sunrise, had been built in a slapdash style that disregarded economy of floor space.

From the shadowy hallway to the left of Sam a gun blared at him. He felt the searing rake of the bullet and fired the Winchester immediately. A voice said, "Christ!" and there were scuttling sounds of withdrawal.

He was hit along the ribs, high on the left side; a heart shot that went inches astray chiefly owing to the shooter's feverish overeagerness. Such frenzy puzzled him. The man could have taken his time and lain in wait. Fighting off a black mist of pain, Sam transferred the rifle to his left hand and drew his six gun. The rifle was not the weapon for a shoot-out at close quarters and, cocking the six gun, he charged at the left hallway.

He had to side-step fast to avoid trampling on Colin DeBray, who lay on the floor with Victoria kneeling beside him at the entrance to the living room. Thinking that DeBray was the shooter, Sam said harshly in response to Victoria's lifting gaze, "It was him or me! He—"

A door to the right of the living room creaked,

and in his own tempest of violence Sam slung a shot that pierced an upper panel of it. Behind the door Tobe Overby snarled, "Damn you, Hatch, you've got your man—what more d'you want? DeBray's the man who stole your father's outfit!"

"I know," Sam said. "I know that now!" He dipped a blank stare at the man lying on the floor. His long search was at its end, yet he felt no uplift of triumph. He had rather liked DeBray, these past few days. "The new foreman of Halfmoon! The good man! My God, DeBray, what made you do it?"

Tobe Overby shouted behind the door, "It wasn't hard to burn four rays on the Halfmoon brand and call it Sunrise! Hatch, you've got it now! Let me get out o' here!"

DeBray said heavily, "First time I ever knew him scared. You got him, Hatch. It was him did the massacre. Him and some Tonks he got mad-drunk. I swear I didn't figure John Heward would have his family along— Stop John Heward from coming up to Desperation Range, that's all I agreed to. . . ."

He was speaking now to Victoria, not to Sam.

"My wife—your mother . . . Eastern girl, used to the best. I wasn't getting ahead fast enough. Wanted to give her everything. So when Tobe Overby came along on the trail and pretty soon talked of how easy I could own the outfit I was driving . . I don't excuse myself, Vic. I finally agreed to it. John Heward was just somebody who'd hired me. He was a severe kind of man, 'cept to his wife and kids. Thought nothin' of bawlin' me out. I was sick of takin' orders, lookin' small in my wife's eyes."

He had reverted to Texas talk, to the drawling accent and the clipping of g's common to Texans.

"I ain't tall. Your mother is. How I won her I'll never know—"

"She loved you," Victoria said to him.

DeBray rolled his head, and a shudder passed through him. "Maybe I was the best she could find in this neck o' the woods. I was young, full o' vinegar. Her family failed in business, went back East. She stayed. With me. God, how happy I was then! But then the Heward business came along. You were about five-six years old, Vic. I took to drinkin'. Maybe I talked in my sleep, I dunno. She left me—"

Tobe Overby, not hearing DeBray's words through the door and persisting in his effort to distract Sam, shouted, "DeBray was laying to cut you down! We fell out over it. He tried to gun me in the back, and I shot him!"

Fighting for breath, DeBray gasped, "He's a liar and a snake! He's sent the whole outfit trailing off. Last night he pulled an all-out raid on Circle K. He was fixin' to clear out and—take you with him, Vic—"

Looking down at the dying man's fading eyes

and at Victoria's white and stricken face, Sam could almost have wished that he had never come to Sunrise, that the truth had lain forever buried. The attempt to bushwhack him, the anxiety of DeBray and Overby lest he be taken to Fort Reno, the reasons behind many things, large and small, grew clear to him now but gave him scant satisfaction. Had he disliked DeBray and had there not been Victoria, he might have suspected the truth much sooner.

A swelling rumble outside roused him out of somber reflections. Then Tobe Overby was yelling desperately, "It's Circle K! Hatch, I'm coming in—don't shoot!" The door banged wide open. Overby came in, holding his rifle above his head. "We've got to pair up against 'em! Krahn's out for your blood as well as mine!"

"I'd as soon pair up with a rattlesnake!" Sam grated at him. But Overby leaped to a window, poking his rifle out, and Sam couldn't quite bring himself to shoot him in the back.

Sam looked out the front door and saw them, Krahn and his Circle K crew of tough hands boiling through the gate into the yard. Their raving temper could be judged by the way they rode in, like a storming bunch of bandits, their plunging horses jostling each other, the foremost riders opening fire as soon as they thundered within six gun range.

Tobe Overby's rifle cracked. Now that he was

caught short on the getaway, Overby had regained his chill nerve, a sneering and humorless grin on his saturnine face. He would not throw in as long as he had a chance left.

A rider lost rhythm with his saddle, jolting and swaying, all ungainly. It served only to heighten the violence of the rest, and a roar of gunfire sprayed the house, sending Sam back from the doorway, Overby ducking below the window, with broken glass showering down on him. Then Krahn, in soiled white linen suit and planter's hat, surged to the lead, swinging an arm over from side to side, and the riders fanned out and split into two groups that swept left and right around the house, shooting into it.

They were yelling and cursing, mad to collect vengeance in full for last night's shambles. Sam, with the idea of gaining for Victoria a safe-conduct out of the house lest the indiscriminate firing take her as victim, sang out, "Hold off! A woman in here!"

His voice battered vainly against the rabid uproar. The attackers blasted every window as they streamed by, deafened by their own racket, and Sam gave up that attempt for the moment, hoping to renew it when the onslaught settled down to its final grim business. For this, he knew from the berserk savagery of it, was not a hit-and-run raid. This was a wipe-out.

SIXTEEN

They started with the barn. The driverless buckboard careened out into the yard, its team bucking and twisting, kicking the vehicle apart. Overby's spooked sorrel followed, and after that, the white mare joined the runaways, her head jerking as she kept stepping on her own reins. Smoke began pouring from the barn, at first curling lazily in the windless air, then rising, the heat of fire creating an updraft.

The commissary building was next. Half a dozen Circle K men broke the door down, and inside they must have splashed coal oil around and lighted it. They tumbled out again hastily, lugging five-gallon cans, flame licking at their heels.

After that, the bunkhouses, oil thrown at them and set afire. The men spread out, and soon every outbuilding had its growing blaze. By that time, the barn was a mammoth bonfire, with bulging walls, and its roof collapsed inward and sent up a great billow of crackling sparks. Something exploded inside the commissary and blew out half its front, and stored boxes of ammunition went to popping like hundreds of firecrackers.

Sunrise was doomed, but the Circle K raiders were not yet finished with their job of total destruction. They had saved the house until last, and its turn had come; and now a man carrying a five-gallon can ran at the rear of it.

Sam, on watch in the kitchen, snapped off a low shot that spilled the running man to his knees. The man cried out, wincing, and a pair of riders converged on him. One of the riders grasped the wounded man, but the other leaned far over and hooked his fingers into the strap handle of the can. Reining his horse hard around, that rider slung the can on at the house. The speed of his turn and his lifting force as he came upright in saddle brought the can sailing the full distance. It struck the kitchen door a shattering blow and evidently burst open from the impact. Oil seeped in under the door.

"They've got to light it yet!" he muttered. But even as he spoke, through the smoke that clouded the yard he made out figures of men picking up burning pieces of planks scattered from the collapsed barn.

Victoria came into the kitchen. She stood behind him at the broken window and said, "The north side of the house is on fire!"

He turned his head to her. It was all over, then. Hiding his hopelessness from her, he said, "Then we have to get out—"

Something thumped softly outside the window. As he turned to look, a bursting sheet of flame curtained the window before him. An accurately thrown ember had ignited the coal oil. It scorched his face and drove him back into Victoria, and without another word they hurried to the front room. The kitchen would be ablaze in minutes.

The front room was filling with smoke. Crouched at a window, Tobe Overby blindly pumped shots from his rifle. The rifle clicked empty, and he cast it aside, saying in a thin and near-tremulous snarl, "They're all gathering here in front, but I can't hardly see 'em now!" Heavy smoke swirled around the house, and he made a futile batting motion with his hand, as if to brush it away. "How's it at the back?"

"Burning," Sam said.

"They're waiting for us to run out!"

"Sure—" Sam took Victoria by an arm. "You've got to go now."

"My father—"

"Nothing to be done for him. He's dead. You've got to go before the smoke gets too thick for them to see you're a woman." He guided her to the open front door and stood the Winchester against the wall.

The smoke, inside and outside, was troublesomely thick. He peered out, and his smarting eyes could barely distinguish hazy shapes of waiting men. In their itch to kill they could easily make a bad mistake, shoot at a moving blur before detecting a woman's dress.

He placed himself behind Victoria, his hands

cupped about her waist. “I’m going to help you off to a fast start, so you’ll clear the smoke in a second. Soon’s they see you’re a woman—”

“But if they don’t—?”

“It’s a risk,” he granted. “Ready, now!” In her fear she had forgotten what awaited him, and he gave a small thought to her oversight and said, “I’ll be along in a minute.”

Then he raised the loudest and most penetrating shout he could muster: *“A woman coming out! A woman! Hold your fire!”*

He lifted Victoria by her waist and sent her flying forward through the smoke.

There was the tense instant of seeing her sail across the porch, her feet not touching it until she was well out beyond the door, as though she performed a remarkable standing jump. Momentum carrying her onward, she then did what she never would have done of her own accord. She cleared the porch steps in a single bound, lost footing at the bottom, and landed rolling in a wild flutter of skirts that nobody could mistake as anything but feminine.

Not a shot had been fired at her. There had hardly been enough time between flying exit and fall. Expelling a deep breath of relief, Sam automatically tensed up again at the opening note of a brazen noise.

Amazingly the noise evolved into the short and rapid blaring of a bugle. It was the first he had heard since his stripling days of outwitting army units sent to capture Tall Horse and his band of fugitives. He had forgotten that such things had ever existed.

Tobe Overby came up out of his crouch. "Soldiers!" he said, peering at Sam in the smoke. "They've got their uses," he added. Swift calculation brought the chill glimmer back into his eyes, and he half turned his body, as if for a last look at dead DeBray. Fire belched from both short hallways, breeding further flames to join those eating through the north wall. The heat in the front room was growing unbearable.

Guessing at Overby's thought, Sam would not present his back to the man. Two people—Victoria and himself—possessed knowledge of Overby's crimes. Victoria might choose silence rather than befoul her dead father's name by divulging his part in that murderous robbery of twenty years ago. Or her story might be discounted, laid to hysteria. . . .

On his right side, the side hidden from Sam, Overby felt at his holstered gun. Divining the move, Sam touched his own with the tips of his fingers, forcing his eyes to stay open in the heat and smoke. Overby turned his head toward him, and with the fire glaring on their sweaty, smoke-blackened faces, they blinked at each other, both stifling off wracking coughs.

Apparently throwing in, Overby lifted his

right hand, empty, saying, "I'm getting out!" Scratching his belly, he made to pass Sam and make it to the door, all the while reaching for the .41 hidden in his shirt.

Reflection of firelight, shifting, contracting to a pin point on the blue-metal shoulder of a fluted cylinder, in its turn pinpointed Sam's undivided distrust and hatred of this man. He glimpsed the round black muzzle tilting at him, Overby holding the hide-out pistol flat across his belly for a side shot at point-blank range.

Sam back-stepped fast, right hand in stroke, the discharge of the pistol tugging at a fold of his shirt front. Overby twisted with frantic speed to make good on the second try, and as he came around he all but chested Sam's rising gun.

Sam fired into him. Twice.

Out front, the metallic voice of Colonel Buskirk pierced the crackling roar of the burning house: "Drop that shooting and come out of there!"

For a few seconds longer Sam stood looking down at Tobe Overby on the floor, feeling spent, suddenly so weary that nothing of all this mattered any more. An aching sickness fogged his brain, and the thought that clung to him concerned the stage station and its occupants. Overby lay unmoving, mouth and eyes open. Sam stumbled out to the porch and down the steps, where two troopers took him by his arms and led him clear.

• • •

Colonel Buskirk used a tone of quiet irony when he asked Sam, "What did Overby tell me your name was?" And when Sam couldn't for the life of him recall it, the colonel nodded: "I'm more certain you're Hatch! In a way you look more like my man now!"

He had shot questions at Krahn and his men before ordering them off. It did not surprise him that they were here in open war, taking reprisal for last night's raid on Circle K. Discovering that his movements were not followed by spies and that therefore the boomers had probably been called in to gang up for some purpose, he had doubled back with his cavalry detachment, smelling mischief. He would send a troop on the trail of the stolen herd, he told Krahn, and telegraph an alarm to all forts in the Territory. He gave the Circle K bunch a scathing lecture on the subject of taking the law into their own hands, and they departed somewhat subdued.

Now he studied Sam's appearancc. Sam bore marks of drastic trouble, his battered face scorched and blackened, hair and eyebrows singed, and his charred shirt had split wide open to reveal the bandage on his chest as well as a red furrow along his ribs. The colonel in his time had seen many men in bad shape. He spoke to the lieutenant:

"Give this man a stiff drink from the medic

case and have a bucket of water drawn for him. I want him fit to travel to Fort Reno with us."

While this was being done, the colonel, watching Sam for a change of expression, said musingly, "Hatch . . . h'm! It occurs to me now that the son of old Tall Horse had a name something on that order. The same man Dr. Dwyer spoke of as having met down near the Mexican border. A shaman, like his father. H'm! What *was* his name? A Sioux name meaning—" Then breaking off, he inquired with impersonal politeness, "Yes, Miss DeBray?"

Victoria had come up to him. White-faced, her dress torn and smudged and her hair in disarray, yet giving an impression of strict correctness, she said, "Colonel, this is Mr. Heward, the owner of Sunrise!"

Colonel Buskirk regarded her, his eyes glacial in a slowly reddening face. After a full minute he found his voice and made a powerful attempt to hold it to a moderate pitch. "I have known this man as Hatch, I swear! Also as Williams, a—a horse-breaker here! Now his name is Heward, and all of a sudden he's the new owner! My dear Miss DeBray—!"

She shook her head. "Not new. He has been the rightful owner for twenty years."

Her tone and manner, carrying conviction, visibly shook the colonel's skepticism. And, sensing the existence of a shameful secret here in her words, perhaps with his sharp intelligence he grasped some dim inkling of the truth, for he looked at the gutted buildings and observed, "Not much left to own, is there? Outside of the livestock—"

Washing in the bucket, Sam wiped his eyes and said, "That reminds me. Everything left of Sunrise on hoofs or wheels is trailing off with the crew. Overby's orders. He was out to make himself the owner. He's dead. And DeBray is dead. Overby killed him."

"That's two outfits for the army to bring back, then. God save us, the army gets more work and less thanks—" Letting that go, the colonel asked Victoria brusquely, "Do you swear to the truth of what you just told me, Miss DeBray? I'll want a full statement later."

"I do swear it," she answered. With difficulty she went on, "My father told me himself, before he died, that he and Overby between them—"

"I'll come to Fort Reno any time you want me, Colonel," Sam cut in. "I'll give you the full statement there. I'll tell you the name of Tall Horse's son—adopted son—"

"Adopted? White?" said the colonel very softly, and Sam nodded.

"Yes, sir. I'll tell you what became of him, what he did, what he is going to do with the rest of his life. But not here, not now. At Fort Reno."

Colonel Buskirk's response was an emphatic,

"Do that, Mr. Heward! It should air out a mystery or two!"

"It should," Sam agreed. "There's nobody alive to be hurt by it any more—"

And yet, he thought later while riding to the stage station, Victoria was alive and she was hurt. She would get over it, yes, but she was hurt now.

She was going back East for good, and the colonel would provide her with an escort to the railroad. At their parting she had said to Sam, "It is all yours, everything that is left of Sunrise. There is banked money— No, don't shake your head. Do you imagine I could keep anything of Sunrise property—now? Knowing what I do? No, no!" And she shuddered. "I shall have the lawyers draw up whatever papers are necessary, at once!"

"But you—what will you—?"

"My mother has an income. Perhaps I shall—marry." Then earnestly: "Things never could have worked out right—between us. Could they, Sam? Because my father—"

And he had slowly shaken his head. It never could have worked out. And not for that reason alone.

Dr. Dwyer was suffering a catastrophic hang-over when Sam gave him the briefest possible account of the day's events, and for the time being the one solid fact that lodged in his befuddled consciousness was that Sam now owned Sunrise. Too sick and trembly to feel overwhelming surprise at anything short of good health, the doctor groaned that hc couldn't stand the smell of cows.

"I've a lot to do," Sam said, "after the outfit's brought back. Got to pick up a new crew. And got to scout up a new range location somewhere outside the Territory. Colonel Buskirk says it'll be thrown open to settlement for sure."

"We could try Wyoming," Dwyer mumbled. "Or Montana. Or New Mexico. Or—"

"We?"

"Wouldn't leave me behind, would you, after all I've done for you? I'll quit drinking. You rope me down if I ever again—"

"I'll have enough to do," Sam said. "Why should I go to that trouble trying to keep you sober?"

Dwyer reflected painfully. "The girls need me. I can go along as their teacher."

"Well, that's truc. They like you, God knows why. So count yourself in. Where are they? Didn't see them in the station when I came in. Thought they'd be in here."

"They were. Don't know how long ago." Remembering something with a nervous start, Dwyer raised bloodshot eyes to Sam: "They were like ghosts, poor kids. Capi had a bruise on her face. Was it you?"

Sam said harshly, "I'd kill any man who did it!"

Dwyer flinched. "Goddam, you're a black big devil!" he muttered. "A damn sight darker than she is, come to that. Her skin's like ivory, but yours is more like the bark of a . . ." But Sam was gone.

Capi and Naka were not anywhere on the stage station, and in dread anxiety Sam called their names. There came no answering halloo, no sound at all. If they were bathing in the stream they would have heard him and responded, but he jumped on the bay and rode down to the stream, calling out again.

"Capi! Naka! Where are you?"

Nor were they there. Not a sign of them, not a wet rock, or a dress spread on a bush; nothing. Yet they understood absolutely that they had to stay close to the stage station. He had impressed it upon them, and so had Dwyer.

Alarm surging through him, Sam started back to the station to try picking up their tracks, and in sweeping a look all around upland for sight of the two, he spied a plume of smoke. It was not in the south, where a gray haze hung over the burned-out buildings of Sunrise. This was north, in the hills, in the near distance, rising from up the arroyo where the wagon was hidden.

While he stared at it, a black speck—charred

canvas or paper—floated in ascent with the smoky spiral. Dread drove a cold knife into his heart and, reining the bay hard about, he lashed the startled animal to a dead run.

Pounding up the crooked arroyo, Sam knew the agony of mingled certainty and suspense. It was indeed the wagon burning, fiercely burning. Above the thud of the bay's hoofs on the sandy floor of the arroyo he heard the popping of the wagon's dry old timbers. He rounded the last bend, and there it was, blazing, brush piled around and under it. The odor of burning hide filled the air. From the bed of the wagon, from the fiery load in it, a series of colored flames spurted, blue and green. The bay horse dug hoofs in a squatting halt, spooked witless, and came up rearing and twisting as Sam lit from the saddle.

Between Sam and the burning wagon stood Capi and Naka, facing him.

They wore their soft buckskins, beaded moccasins, and headbands. Their hair hung forward in thick twin braids. Erect, impassive, they met Sam's look. Their eyes they could not discipline as well under his gaze, for Naka was a child and Capi a young maid; two girls standing up to desolation together, as terribly alone as during the days of the dead village.

Sam looked into despairing grief, unutterable woe. He asked "Why?" and a choking in his throat roughened his voice.

Capi's hands, those betraying small hands, moved slightly, fingers curling. Her oval face stayed masked, the line from temple to chin a delicate and unbroken curve, lips firm. As the doctor had said, her skin was like ivory; its texture had the same fineness as that of the child and usually glowed softly with an inner warmth, but the warmth was missing now, the blood having receded.

She spoke in unadulterated Arapaho, using with a quiet and unaffected dignity the timeless *Hinanatina* phrases of ceremonious politeness. For this was a grave occasion, a black day of heartbreaking decision, and she was a well-brought-up girl whose manners must present even more impeccable decorum, the deeper her inner chaos.

The rounded vowels and clear consonants and small shadings of gutturals slipped from her lips with the flowing eloquence of a rehearsed speech. And Sam, hearing from her the answer to his single-word question and trapped by her steadfast formality, did not interrupt.

He wished, she said, to belong with his own kind, a white man among white people, and that was right. It was a right and proper desire. Very well. *Nunwe* . . .

But there was the sacred parfleche of Tall Horse, and Sam was bound to it, sworn to protect it, by his oath to Tall Horse. The parfleche was an

Indian thing, a burden upon his wish. That was bad. It was bad for him.

Therefore did she burn the sacred parfleche. *Ma-ya, na* . . . And all other things of his Indian past also, thus freeing him. And this was good, this was *napave.*

And she and Naka, being also burdens upon his wish . . .

"We go now," Capi ended, taking Naka's hand.

Where they could go she had no idea. It didn't matter. They were unwanted. They would go.

Sam's throat ached, and it took him a few moments to loosen its constriction so that he could speak. Capi's forlorn line of reasoning made plain to him his shortcomings. He had failed her, and failed Naka.

Preoccupied with his two obsessions—to regain his white heritage and to track down the white renegade responsible for the massacre of his family—he had tended to regard Capi and Naka with some compassion as objects of his duty, less than paramount to his wishes. Since coming here he had all but rejected them, at least by his actions, spending much of his time with Victoria DeBray. It had remained for Victoria unwittingly to awaken him.

He said huskily and very gently, "Don't go. Don't leave me—"

Naka was first to move, taking a hesitant step toward him, her face lighting up at the look in his eyes, as though a whole new world might be opening before her. Throwing off a curious shyness, Sam reached down and fingered one of her braids, and, letting his hand slide on as carefully as with a skittish colt, he curved it to the smooth nape of her neck and drew her to him.

"Naka, you're my little girl. My own little girl. I won't ever let you down again."

He felt the freely forgiving pressure of the child's arm sliding about his waist. He looked over her head at Capi and said again, "Don't go." And then: "I need you." At last he got the words out that he wanted to say to her:

"I love you, Capi."

The oval face lost every bit of its impassive mask, the glow returned richly to the ivory skin; grief and woe fled from the radiance in her eyes. With a happy sob of thankfulness Capi came rushing to his arms and, deep within Sam, a tender warmth moved to meet hers. A new and joyous brightness of spirit promised him that he was about to begin living. The coming days and years offered splendid life, free of bitter search, and he would live it, really and truly live it.

Books are produced in the United States using U.S.-based materials

Books are printed using a revolutionary new process called THINKtech™ that lowers energy usage by 70% and increases overall quality

Books are durable and flexible because of smythe-sewing

Paper is sourced using environmentally responsible foresting methods and the paper is acid-free

Center Point Large Print
600 Brooks Road / PO Box 1
Thorndike, ME 04986-0001 USA

(207) 568-3717

US & Canada:
1 800 929-9108
www.centerpointlargeprint.com